Samuel Cox, Samuel Cox

The private letters of St. Paul and St. John

Samuel Cox, Samuel Cox

The private letters of St. Paul and St. John

ISBN/EAN: 9783743491427

Printed in Europe, USA, Canada, Australia, Japan

Cover: Foto ©Raphael Reischuk / pixelio.de

Manufactured and distributed by brebook publishing software
(www.brebook.com)

Samuel Cox, Samuel Cox

The private letters of St. Paul and St. John

PRIVATE LETTERS.

THE

Private Letters

OF

ST. PAUL AND ST. JOHN.

BY THE

REV. SAMUEL COX.

LONDON: ARTHUR MIALL,
18, BOUVERIE STREET, E.C.

1867.

PREFATORY NOTE.

THE contents of this little book were originally delivered as week-evening Lectures in the ordinary course of my ministry. I have added a few notes to make them more complete, but have not attempted to change their structure. So far as my reading enables me to judge, they contain all that is known of the three Private Letters included in the New Testament, all that is requisite to enable the English reader to judge of their worth and claims, with this exception.—I have not, simply because I wished to confine myself to Exposition, discussed the authorship or the canonicity of these Epistles. Of the authorship of the Epistle to Philemon, indeed, or of its inspiration, there is no grave or general doubt. But, if any of them are ignorant of the fact, my readers ought perhaps to be told, that the two Letters of St. John have often been denied a place in the Canon; and that by some learned and devout critics these Letters, in common with the Gospel of St. John, have been attributed to a certain Presbyter of the Church of Ephesus, and not to John the Apostle. On these two points I can only say that, after carefully weighing all the evidence that has been adduced, I hold strongly to the more general conviction of the Church, that these Epistles are the work of the beloved Apostle; and that they have an unshaken claim to their place among the Canonical Scriptures.

CONTENTS.

I.

ST. PAUL'S LETTER TO PHILEMON.

I.

THE EPISTLE TO PHILEMON.

PAUL, a prisoner of Jesus Christ, and Timotheus the brother, to Philemon our beloved friend and fellow-labourer,

2. And to our sister Appia, and to Archippus our fellow-soldier, and to the church in thy house :

3. Grace to you, and peace from God our Father, and from our Lord Jesus Christ.

4. I thank my God that I hear of thy love and of the faith which thou hast toward the Lord Jesus, and toward all the saints ;

5. Always making mention of thee in my prayers,

6. That the fellowship of thy faith may become

Vers. 4—6. This sentence runs in a very involved form in the Greek, though its sense is clear. Literally rendered, it would read thus : (4) " I thank my God, always making mention of thee in my prayers, (5) hearing of thy love and of the faith which thou hast toward the Lord Jesus and unto all the saints, (6) in order that the fellowship (or the communion) of thy faith may become an energy in the full recognition of every good thing which is in us, unto (*i. e.*, to the honour of) Christ Jesus." As I read the verses, however, that for which the Apostle gives thanks is the faith and love which he hears that Philemon has evinced; and that for

B

effectual in the full knowledge of every good thing which is in us, unto Christ Jesus.

7. For I have had much joy and consolation in thy love, because the hearts of the saints have been refreshed by thee, brother.

8. Wherefore, though I might be much bold to enjoin upon thee that which is befitting, yet, for love's sake, I rather beseech thee.

9. Being such an one,—as aged Paul, and now also a prisoner of Christ Jesus,

10. I beseech thee for my own child whom I have begotten in my bonds, for Onesimus,

which he prays is that Philemon's faith may grow into a completer fellowship with his own. To bring out this sense I have transposed the members of the sentence as in the text. I may also remark that it seems impossible, without a paraphrase, to give the force of the two Greek prepositions in the phrase, "the faith which thou hast *toward* the Lord Jesus and *toward* (or *unto*) all the saints." The meaning seems to be, that the faith for which the Apostle gives thanks is the faith which Philemon reposes in the Lord Jesus, and the existence of which he manifests and demonstrates by the kindly services he renders to the saints: the inference being, that faith in Christ, unless shown in works of neighbourly charity, is dead; that kind deeds are the logical result and characteristic manifestation of faith in Jesus. And into what English preposition can one crowd so large a meaning as that?

Ver. 10. "*Being such an one:*" i. e., being one who is disposed to waive rights rather than to enforce them, who would rather entreat and persuade than exercise even an admitted authority, I do not command, as I might, but beseech thee, pleading my age and hapless estate as a prisoner, that you may be the more ready to relent and grant my prayer.

"*As aged Paul.*" What age was Paul when he wrote this letter? It is impossible to determine; all attempts to fix the date of his birth having failed. He may have been nearly sixty, he could hardly have been less, or much less, than fifty years of age: but though an ordinary man of fifty could hardly plead age, yet a man broken by so many labours, perils, sorrows, cares, as St. Paul, and exhausted by his fervid genius, may very well have been far older than his years.

11. Who was once unprofitable to thee, but now is profitable both to thee and to me,

12. Whom I send back. Do thou receive him that is as my own heart;

13. Whom I wished to have retained with me, that, in thy stead, he might minister unto me in the bonds of the gospel;

14. But without thy consent I would do nothing, that thy goodness should not be as by compulsion but voluntary.

15. For, peradventure, he departed from thee for a time to this very end, that thou mightest have him as thine own for ever;

16. No longer only as a slave, but as more than a slave, a brother beloved, very dear to me, but how much more to thee, both in the flesh and in the Lord.

17. If thou art in fellowship with me, welcome him as myself;

18. And if he hath wronged thee, or oweth thee aught, put that to my account—

19. I, Paul, write this with my own hand—I will repay it: for I care not to remind thee that thou owest me even thine own self.

20. Yea, brother, let me have profit of thee in the Lord: refresh my heart in Christ.

21. I write to thee relying on thy obedience, knowing that thou wilt do even more than I say.

22. But at the same time provide me a lodging,

for I hope that, through your prayers, I shall be given to you.

23. There salute thee Epaphras my fellow-prisoner in Christ Jesus ;

24. Marcus, Aristarchus, Demas, Lucas, my fellow-labourers.

25. The grace of our Lord Jesus Christ be with your spirit.

The private letters of public men have a very special worth and interest for us. Of all documents, perhaps, these yield the most significant and accurate indices of character. In these we see the writer in undress, not in his robes of state ; in his natural posture, not in any attitude struck to catch the general eye ; as he was to his friends and

---

Ver. 23. *Epaphras* is mentioned first probably because, as he was a member of the Colossian Church (Col. iv. 12, 13), he would be the personal friend of Philemon.

Ver. 24. *Mark*, "the cousin of Barnabas " (Col. iv. 10), about whom , there had once sprung up so sharp a contention between Barnabas and Paul (Acts xv. 36—39). *Aristarchus*, the Macedonian, who sailed with Paul in the "ship of Adramyttium " (Acts xxvii. 2), and who was now his "fellow-prisoner" (Col. iv. 10). *Demas*, who though now with the imprisoned Apostle, afterward forsook him, "having loved this present world " (2 Tim. iv. 10). *Lucas*, or Luke, "the beloved physician " (Col. iv. 14), and the Evangelist of the Gentiles, who, in all proba-- bility, was at this time the secretary or amanuensis of St. Paul.

intimates, not as he "appeared unto men." The
discovery of letters written in the abandon of familiar intercourse, and not meant to see the light, has
often changed, and sometimes reversed, the popular
estimate of men once thought to be very great or
very holy: while, on the other hand, the publication
of letters such as these has, at times, greatly raised
their author in the public esteem, his unstudied
friendly utterances disclosing a delicate grace and
beauty, or a largeness of mind and loftiness of aim,
or a devout tenderness of spirit, which he never
altogether succeeded in expressing while under the
eye of the world.

If, therefore, we had only St. Paul's public utterances, such, for instance, as his defence before King
Agrippa, or his magnificent oration on Mars' Hill,
or his pathetic farewell to the Elders of Ephesus,
or even the Epistles he addressed to the Churches;
—if we had only these, although we should still be
able to form a tolerably large and accurate conception of the man, for more than most men St. Paul
wore his heart upon his sleeve, we should nevertheless lack some criteria, some indications and

"notes" of character, which it would be well that
we should have. For Paul, the Apostle of the
Gentiles, and, after the Lord Jesus, the greatest
teacher of truth the world has seen, naturally fills
a large space in the thoughts of Gentiles whose
"open eyes desire the truth." We think of him
much and often ; and it is of no slight importance
that we should form an accurate and complete conception of his character. And really it is hard to
say *what* that would really help us to such a conception has been withheld. We have, for the New
Testament, a singularly full biography of him by
St. Luke : nay, if we piece together the personal
allusions scattered through his Epistles, we have
an autobiography which covers all the essential
features and critical occasions of his life. We
have his speeches before kings and governors, and
before large public audiences, both of those who
believed in, and those who mocked at, Jesus and
the Resurrection. We have his Epistles to the
Churches, which expound his whole system of
thought, and disclose his method of instruction.
And, finally, we have the Letters he addressed

to private friends, such as Timothy, Titus,* and
Philemon. There is no lack, therefore, of materials
out of which to build up a true conception of
the great Apostle, though I fear that many
of his letters, letters which we should have
been very glad to read, are irrecoverably lost. If
we do not know the man, in his habit, as he lived,
it is simply because we have not mastered his biography and autobiography, his speeches and sermons,
his private Letters and public Epistles.

I.—Let us take up and examine one of these
Letters,—the letter he wrote to his friend Philemon,
about his friend Onesimus. Naturally, one of the
first questions we ask about it is this : Does it correspond, in tone and spirit, with his public Epistles ?
Does it reveal the very man whom we have so often
heard teaching and preaching in the name of the
Lord Jesus ? Or is there, as sometimes happens,

---

* The Epistles to Timothy and Titus, the *Pastoral* Epistles, can hardly
be ranked as private letters; for, though written to private friends, there is
a breadth of tone about them which indicates that they were meant for a
larger public than the friends to whom they were addressed, or than even
the pastors of that time. Indeed, there are no letters in the New Testament which are strictly *private* letters, save the three discussed in this
volume.

a wide difference between the private man and the
public character ?   I think we shall find that there
is no such difference.   I think we shall find that
the private letter shows us a man as courteous, as
large-minded, as ardent, as devout, as that Apostle
whose public labours and utterances have given us
so lofty a conception of both his character and his
genius.   But before we can answer this question to
advantage, we must a little consider under what
conditions this Letter was written ; we must also
learn what we can of the two men, Onesimus and
Philemon, whom it chiefly concerned.

When he wrote this Letter, St. PAUL was a
prisoner in imperial Rome—it contains at least three
allusions to his *bonds*—awaiting the sentence of the
Emperor Nero.   He had appealed to Cæsar, claim-
ing his right as a Roman citizen ; and to Cæsar he
was sent.   In Rome he had to suffer the torture of
" the law's delay."   The official documents connected with his case had probably been lost in the
shipwreck off Malta ; it would be long before
duplicates could be obtained.   The prosecutors and

witnesses had to be brought from Syria to Italy, a tedious and perilous journey. Nero was full of caprice, and so averse to business that it was only at rare intervals he could be got to hear a suit and give his verdict. For these and the like reasons, the trial of Paul was postponed for two years. During this interval, through the humanity of the Prætorian Prefect Burrhus, St. Paul, as Luke tells us,* was allowed to dwell in " his own hired house." But we must not suffer St. Luke's phrase to mislead our thoughts. This " hired house " was by no means the comfortable residence one might suppose it to have been. The stately marble palace of the Emperor, like the other patrician mansions of Rome, was surrounded by wooden huts and cabins tenanted by the innumerable train of slaves, minions, and freedmen who were retained for the service of the palace and its inmates. And it was in one of these miserable dens that the Apostle was permitted to reside, instead of being cast into the vast horrible dungeons beneath the palace floor. Night and day, moreover, he was chained to soldier after soldier of

* Acts xxviii. 30.

the Imperial guard, no moment of privacy allowed him; and was, no doubt, often treated with insolence, if not with violence, by the rude mercenaries. With his right wrist chained to the soldier's left wrist, he sat for " two whole years " in his wooden hut, teaching all who came to him, and winning some of his guards, nay, even some of the minions and parasites of the Court—for he speaks of his successes in the Prætorium*—to the faith of Christ. " The care of all the churches " was upon him: messengers were constantly arriving and departing

---

* The Epistle to the Philippians, like that to Philemon, was written during St. Paul's Roman imprisonment. And in this Epistle (Phil. i. 12, 13), he assures his friends at Philippi that his "circumstances have fallen out unto the furtherance of the Gospel; so that my bonds have become manifest in Christ *in the whole Prætorium*, and to all the rest." The meaning of the phrase, "in the whole Prætorium," is disputed. It may mean either the palace of the Emperor, or the barrack (or camp) of the Prætorian guards. If we must choose between the two, I should prefer the former interpretation, since (Phil. iv. 22), the Apostle closes the Epistle with a salutation from "*they that are of Cæsar's household*" to their brethren at Philippi; and thus proves that he had converts in the palace. But, to a certain extent at least, the two interpretations may be reconciled. For the Prætorians furnished the body-guard to the Emperor; this body-guard had a barrack in the precincts of the palace, as well as a camp outside the city. And it was, probably, in one of the huts composing, or connected with, this barrack, that St. Paul was confined. Both barrack and palace were called the Prætorium; and therefore when Paul speaks of his success in "*the whole* Prætorium," it seems best to understand him as affirming that in both the places which bore this name, in the palace and in the barrack, among the guards and among the retainers of the court, he had found willing hearers of the Gospel of our redemption. Merivale has a good note on this point in his " History of the Romans under the Empire," vol. vi. chap. liv. p. 438.

with messages, or gifts, or letters : and in the intervals of worship and teaching, the fettered Apostle dictated the Epistles he could no longer write, only adding a few words (as in Philemon, ver. 19) with his own hand—a hand so weighted and cramped with the pendant chain that his words were of necessity few, and the letters * he formed with it of necessity "large."

What a picture rises in the mind as one tries to conceive the scene! There, in his wooden cabin, often "crowded" by anxious hearers of the Word, sits a scholar and a gentleman, exhausted by the labours of the day. The lamp shines down on his bald forehead, lights up the keen aquiline features of his oval face, shaded with grey hair,† and glitters from

---

* St. Paul, however, seems always to have written a bold dashing hand. Thus, for instance, writing to the Galatians (chap. vi. 11), he says, "Look ye in what *large letters* I write with mine own hand." The fact has been variously accounted for. Some attribute it to his defective eyesight, others to a nervous palsy, induced by his many sufferings, and especially by his long endurance of chains. Both these causes may have had something to do with the "large" handwriting of the Apostle; but surely Theodore of Mopsuestia comes nearer the mark when he attributes "the boldness of the handwriting to the force of the Apostle's convictions." It was, in all probability, the bold fervent character of the man, even more than any bodily defect, which led him to use "large letters."

† This is no fancy portrait, or, if it be, I am not responsible for it. In all works of early Christian art, and notably in the Roman catacombs, St. Paul is portrayed as of short stature, bald head, bushy eyebrows, pointed beard, clear grey eyes, aquiline nose, and a long oval face.

the armour of the brawny Prætorian who lounges beside him, and from the links of the chain which binds them wrist to wrist. Paul dictates sentence after sentence to Luke, the learned physician, who carries his pen and inkhorn at his waist. He is inditing a letter to his friend Philemon in far-away Phrygian Colossæ, about a runaway slave, pleading for the outcast, promising that if in anything the slave has wronged his master, he, Paul, will be answerable for it. The thought strikes him that the promise will carry more weight with it if written by his own hand. He interrupts the flow of speech; cries, " Here, Luke, give me the reed!" and with benumbed labouring fingers inscribes these words, "I, Paul, write this *with my own hand*—I will repay it."

It is touching—is it not, to think of so great a man in such miserable conditions ? A man so like the Master whom he serves that, while he carries whole races and churches on his heart, he yet has a special love for every wretched outcast who will accept his love; and is not only bent on serving him, but will take thought how he may best serve him, and spare no pains to make his service effectual.

PHILEMON, to whom St. Paul wrote, was probably a native of Colossæ, certainly an inhabitant of
that Phrygian city. We know nothing of him save
that which we learn from the hints given in this
Epistle, as interpreted by the customs and conditions of his time. From these we infer that he
was a large householder, a man of property and
influence, addicted to hospitality, charitable to the
poor, and that he had "a church" in his house,
i.e., gathered his brethren and sisters in Christ together for worship, and for the "feasts" which
then accompanied worship. "The sister Appia,"
mentioned in ver. 2, was probably, as the early
Greek commentators affirm, the wife of Philemon.
"Archippus, our fellow-soldier," was a minister of
the Gospel at Colossæ; for, in his Epistle to the
Colossians,* St. Paul writes, "Say to Archippus,
take heed to the ministry which thou receivedst in
the Lord, that thou fulfil it." Probably too, as the
commentators suppose, he was the son of Philemon
and Appia, and the minister of the church in their

* Colossians iv. 17. It is not improbable, as some of the commentators
infer from the warning yet inspiriting tone of this message, that Archippus
was a young man *recently* called to the ministry of the Word.

house.   These conjectures and traditions are, at
least, so far confirmed by St. Paul's letter as this :
that, in writing on a matter so strictly private as the
conversion and return of a runaway slave, it is not
at all likely that the Apostle would send special
greeting to any but Philemon and the members of
his family.

This Colossian householder had received the
Gospel from the lips of St. Paul himself: for Paul
reminds him (ver. 19) that he owed " even his own
self," his own soul, to him ; that is, he had been
converted under the Apostle's ministry.*   The
good seed fell into a good soil: for Philemon became full of the faith which worketh by love (ver.
4) ; the hearts of many of the saints were " refreshed" by his good deeds and kindly help (ver. 7).
Hospitable and charitable, he was also docile, only

---

* This conclusion has been questioned on the ground that St. Paul
never was at Colossæ, that the Church there was founded by Epaphras, not
by the Apostle.   But in an age of commerce and travel, St. Paul must
have preached to many men whose cities he never entered.   A man of
Philemon's position must, in all probability, have been often carried by his
affairs from the Phrygian table-lands, on which Colossæ stood, along the
great road from the Euphrates to Ephesus, which swept close by Colossæ, to
Ephesus the chief port and market of the province.   St. Paul taught three
years at Ephesus.   Is it altogether incredible that Philemon should have
visited the neighbouring city during that time, and there have heard the
good tidings of salvation from the Apostle's lips ?

needing a hint of duty to go beyond the mere claims of duty. "I know," cries Paul, "that thou wilt do even more than I say" (ver. 21).

We may conceive of Philemon, therefore, as one of those Asiatic "lords," or "householders," to whom the Lord Jesus often refers in His parables; as having many slaves to whom he entrusted his goods, according to their several ability to use them; as a *Christian* householder, with a Christian wife, and a son a Christian minister, and a Christian church in his house; as a man of singularly *high* Christian character, full of love and faith and good works.*

Among his slaves was a certain ONESIMUS, a Phrygian by race, a Colossian by birth. In a Christian household, such as that of Philemon, we may be tolerably sure that slavery took its least offensive form; that the rule of the lord, or house-

* Tradition adds to all we know of Philemon, that he was bishop of Colossæ or of Gaza—which is very unlikely—and became a martyr at Rome during the persecution of Nero—which may be true, as also it may not. Theodoret says that his house was still shown in Colossæ in the fifth century after Christ; but I believe that to this very day they profess to show you in Jerusalem the house of that rich man at whose gate lay beggar Lazarus, and possibly the former relic was as genuine, *i e.* as spurious, as is the latter.

holder, was lenient and gracious ; that Onesimus, in common with his fellows, would be fairly treated, and must have had many opportunities of hearing the truth as it is in Jesus. But something in the man, whether a virtue or a vice of blood, revolted from his condition, and rendered him impervious to the hopes and consolations of his master's faith. That Onesimus was a man of good natural ability and disposition seems evident from St. Paul's high appreciation of him : for Paul was no mean judge of men, and he loved Onesimus "as his own heart" (ver. 12); had found his company very " profitable" (ver. 11); and would have liked to retain him as a friend and minister (ver. 13). But, on the other hand, Onesimus was not a prisoner of war ; not, therefore, one of those most miserable of men who, more refined and of a higher spirit and culture than their masters, were, nevertheless, compelled to endure whatever degradation, or insult, or torture they were pleased to inflict upon them. He was a Colossian in the service of a Colossian.*

---

* In the Epistle to the Colossians (iv. 9), St. Paul speaks of Onesimus as " our faithful and beloved brother, *who is one of you,*" *i. e.,* who is of

Probably, therefore, he was a home-born slave, with slaves for his parents, or a man of low class or habits who sold himself into bondage that he might eat bread. I am afraid, too, that Onesimus was a thief. For though it is possible to suppose that the wrong he had done his master was simply that of absconding from his service, yet the allusion in this Letter to the fact that Onesimus was once " unprofitable" to his master (ver. 11); the request, " if he hath wronged thee, or oweth thee aught, put that to my account" (ver. 18); and the promise, "I will repay it" (ver. 19), all seem to point to an embezzlement: they indicate that, allured by the prospect of liberty, and the chance of carrying off a sum which would make his liberty bearable, if not pleasant, Onesimus absconded with money or goods which his master had entrusted to him.

After many wanderings and perils, he arrived in Rome—the crowded metropolis, then as now, being the resort in which all fugitives from law or justice found their best chance of concealment. We can

your race and city, and not simply a member of your Church. So, at least, the best commentators read the phrase.

imagine with what a rabble of criminals, rogues, sharpers, gladiators, and fugitive slaves, Onesimus must have herded in the vile haunts of the imperial city, and how quickly he would squander his booty among them, or be swindled out of it. But, at last, a gracious Providence brought him to St. Paul's hut. Among "the crowd which pressed" on the Apostle " daily," there one day stood the Phrygian slave. His crime, or its evil punitive results, have awakened conscience; the cleansing healing truth comes home to him. As he listens, he repents, converts, and is saved. He tells his story to the Apostle, is taught his sin, and yet comforted with hopes brighter than he had ever known. He devotes himself to the service of the teacher of whom he had learned the way of truth and peace. Paul loves him—loves him so well that he can part with him for his good. He thinks it will be good for Onesimus to go back to his master and atone his trespass. He sends him back with Tychicus, who carries the Epistle to the Colossian Church, while Onesimus bears a letter to Philemon, the Colossian householder,—a letter which, I suppose, Paul thought would never be read except by his friend Philemon, Appia his sister, and his comrade Archippus, but which the Holy Ghost has graciously put into our hands.*

Here, then, we may return to the question with which we started. We may once more ask, Does this private letter correspond, in tone and spirit, with St. Paul's public Epistles? for now we are in a position to reply. We are able to compare the Letter in the hands of Onesimus with the Epistle in the hands of Tychicus—they lie side by side between the covers of the same Book—and to determine whether or not the Apostle is one man in public, and in private another man.

Look at these two Letters, then, and you will see that even in external form there is a close resemblance between them. The Epistle to the Colossians opens with the salutation, " Paul, an Apostle of Jesus Christ by the will of God, and Timotheus the bro-

---

* To all we know of Onesimus, tradition adds that he became Bishop of Berea, in Macedonia ;—curiously enough, hardly a person is mentioned in the New Testament whom eccl. siastical history does *not* make a bishop, or a martyr, or both,—and died in Rome, a martyr to the faith.

ther, to the holy and faithful brethren in Christ at
Colossæ: Grace to you, and peace from God our
Father and the Lord Jesus Christ " (vers. 1, 2). The
Letter to Philemon opens with " Paul, a prisoner of
Jesus Christ, and Timotheus the brother, to Philemon our beloved friend and fellow-labourer : grace
to you, and peace from God our Father and the
Lord Jesus Christ " (vers. 1, 3). In the Epistle
to the Colossians, the salutation is followed by a
thanksgiving, " We give thanks to God, the Father
of our Lord Jesus Christ . . . having heard of your
faith in Christ Jesus, and of *the love which ye have
toward all the saints* " (vers. 3, 4); the thanksgiving is followed by a prayer, " We do not cease
to pray for you, and to make our petition that ye
may be *filled with the knowledge* of His will in all
spiritual wisdom and understanding " (ver. 9).
And in the Letter to Philemon, the salutation is also
followed by a thanksgiving for the very same graces,
" I thank my God that I hear of thy *love,* and of
thy faith which thou hast *toward the Lord Jesus*
and *toward all the saints*" (ver. 4.) : and the thanksgiving is also followed by a prayer for the very same

blessing, " Making mention of thee always in my prayers, that the fellowship of thy faith may become effectual in *the full knowledge* of every good thing " (vers. 5, 6). * In both Epistles there are allusions to St. Paul's bonds, and his chain is lifted in pathetic appeal ; † both close with greetings from the same saints,‡ and with an Apostolic benediction.§

Beneath this similarity of form there lies unity of spirit. Not only in his Epistle to the Colossians, but in all his public appearances and utterances, St. Paul was distinguished by a singular tact and courtesy. He carried himself like a gentleman versed in the best manners of his time, and of all time. This courtesy is very conspicuous in his letter to Philemon, so conspicuous and pervading, indeed, that it was commonly known to our fathers as "the Polite Epistle." For eighteen centuries, by men of all races and schools of thought, it has been admired as a model of composition, unsurpassed, and

---

* The reader, carefully comparing these citations, will discover many minute correspondences of phrase and structure which it was well nigh impossible to bring out in a spoken discourse.

† Compare Col. i. 24, iv. 3, 4, 10, and 18, with Philemon 1, 9, 10, 23.

‡ Compare Col. iv. 10—14, with Phil. 23, 24.

§ Compare Col. iv. 18, with Phil. 25.

well-nigh unapproachable, in its mingled dignity and sweetness. It is impossible, it would be tedious, to go into minute detail, or I could show you that almost every line and every word, every turn of thought and phrase, is governed by an exquisite grace and tact beyond the reach of art. You will gain some sense of the refined courtesy which breathes through every sentence of this Letter, if you simply reflect on the difficulties of the task to which the Apostle addressed himself, and the completeness of his victory over them. He was the common friend of Philemon and Onesimus, each of whom thought the other to have wronged him. He must conciliate Philemon, yet commend Onesimus. He must commend Onesimus, and yet not cloak his fault. He has to affirm the brotherhood of slave and slave-owner, and to ask from a justly-offended master, not only pardon, but fraternal kindness, for a fugitive and criminal slave. He might claim to speak with authority, might be " bold to enjoin, " since Philemon owes him far more than Onesimus owes Philemon ; but he prefers to ask a favour, and " for love's sake to beseech." He hardly likes to allude to his own services; yet how, without some such allusion, which it is equally difficult to make and to avoid, can he get Philemon to feel that he asks less than he has given. He has to point out a duty, but would fain inspire a voluntary act of grace. It is because St. Paul has met these and kindred difficulties with the most sensitive and consummate tact; because by hints, by broken phrases, by half-suggestions, by touches of pathos, and even, as we shall see, by strokes of humour, he has succeeded in conveying all these contradictory moods of thought, without any sacrifice of truth or dignity, or the use of a single phrase at which the captious might take offence, that this letter has been singled out as the purest model of epistolary composition, and has been named by good judges " the Polite Epistle."

How generous, too, and how like the man, is the ardour with which he pleads the cause of the outcast! It is hardly possible to imagine any other Roman gentleman of that time so much as lifting one of his fingers to help a slave, much less a runaway slave who had embezzled his master's property. But how earnestly Paul pleads for him; how his ardour mounts and grows! "I beseech thee for *my own child* whom I have begotten in my bonds, for Onesimus" (ver. 10). "Do thou receive him that is *as my own heart*" (ver. 12), as "*a brother beloved, very dear to me*" (ver. 16). "If thou art in fellowship with me, welcome him *as myself*" (ver. 17). "If he hath wronged thee, or oweth thee aught, *put that to my account. I, Paul, write this with my own hand*"—so earnest am I, so bent on winning grace for him—"*I will repay thee*" (vers. 18, 19). "Yea, brother, *let me have profit of thee : refresh my heart* in Christ" (ver. 20). *I know that thou wilt do even more than I say*" (ver. 21). Is it not beautiful, is it not pathetic, to note the intense beseeching earnestness which trembles in these phrases, to mark the ingenious variations through which love pursues its single prayer? He pleads as for his own son, as for his dearest friend, as for himself, as for his own heart. Could the force of love go further? Is not this the Paul we know— as fervid, as tender, as great of heart while he pleads for this poor outcast as when he pleads for Christ?

Nor, if we remember how even a slight stroke of humour deepens pathos, shall we feel either surprise or regret as we learn that St. Paul's humour* breaks through his most fervent appeals. Our English version gives no hint of the fact. Nor, indeed, is the humour at all profound. It is simply a pun, a play upon words; yet I can conceive that Paul uttered it with a somewhat sad and wistful face. The jest lies in the name of the slave. Onesimus means " profitable " or " useful: " because of the meaning of the word, it was a common name among the slaves of antiquity. In the tenth and eleventh verses of this Letter, Paul writes, " I beseech thee for my own child whom I have begotten in my bonds, for Onesimus "—or, as we should say, for *Profitable*,—" who was once *unprofitable* to thee, but now is *profitable* both to thee and to me." We can hardly pronounce the jest to

---

* A very striking essay might be written on the Humour of St. Paul. There are abundant materials for it. No one at all conversant with his Epistles in the Greek can doubt that a very strong vein of humour ran through his mind, or that he freely used this, as all other gifts, in the service of Christ. In the First Epistle to the Corinthians, for instance, he again and again takes up the admissions or boasts of the Corinthian converts, and holds them in the most ludicrous and absurd lights, that he may shame his readers out of their follies and sins.

be of singular excellence; but St. Paul finds it such an excellent good jest, that he recurs to it in the twentieth verse, " Yea, brother, let me have *profit* of thee." But whatever we may think of this play on words—and even the greatest wits sometimes stoop to these familiar touches—it is surely pleasant to conceive of the Apostle as thus unbending in his familiar intercourse with his friends, and as ingeniously blunting the edge of Philemon's resentment, by talking, as John Bunyan might have done, of " Master Profitable, who was once unprofitable, but who will henceforth deserve his name."

Hardly enough, perhaps, has been made of this point—that the humour of the Apostle covers his tact. He has to refer to the sin—the embezzlement—of Onesimus, that he may ask pardon for it. But how shall he refer to it so as at once to hurt the repentant slave as little as he may, and to placate his offended master? Philemon, as he recalled the offence of Onesimus, would be apt to frown. If the Apostle could so touch that offence as to make Philemon smile, much would be gained. Philemon could hardly but smile at the notion of

"Profitable" having been "unprofitable;" and thus the Apostle would have gained his end with him. He would also have gained his end with Onesimus: for how could his wound be more gently touched? how, if his offence must be recalled, could it be recalled more lightly and tenderly?

Nor must we omit to note the pure and high devotion which characterizes St. Paul's most familiar talk no less than his public utterances. Here, he is only writing, on a private affair, to a personal friend; he unbends into an innocent jest: but he opens his Letter with salutations and thanksgivings and prayers, and closes it with a benediction, as lofty and devout as though he were writing to a church on the profoundest mysteries of the Faith. The main body or substance of his Letter, moreover, is, as we shall presently see, most devout and religious. Under all its courtesies and jests and pathetic personal appeals, there lies this great argument—and it is *the* argument of the Letter—that there is a Christian "fellowship," or communion, of which Paul and Philemon and Onesimus are all members ; that if this fellowship is an effectual energy, and not a mere name, they are all brethren; that this new Christian relation overrides all other relations ; that in Christ Jesus there is neither Jew nor Greek, neither Asiatic nor Roman, neither master nor slave, bond nor free, but all are brethren because *He* is Brother to all. It is this underlying argument, which only crops up to the surface now and then, that makes the Apostolic appeal so cogent, so ardent, so pathetic, so effective.

And it is only this Christian fellowship, and our deep sense of it, which will give the right tone to all our speech, the right form to all our conduct. We are apt to forget this, to think too little of the shaping spirit of our life and too much of its outward forms. Take an illustration suggested by our theme. As we read this Letter to Philemon, we can hardly fail to ask ourselves, "How is it that Christian men no longer correspond in this style ? When *we* write to a brother in the Faith, we send him no Christian salutation or benediction, no thanksgiving for the good already wrought in him by the grace of God, no prayer that the fellowship of our faith may grow more effectual and sweep a wider range. We hardly ever do that : yet St. Paul seems to have done it habitually, in his private notes no less than in his public correspondence." True, my brethren. Nevertheless, how foolish it would be of us to copy his forms of correspondence instead of seeking to share his spirit ! There are still whole races of men—most of the Oriental races— who use these devout forms as habitually as St. Paul himself, and are in nothing the better for it, often the worse. Let me read you a modern letter * of this kind, omitting only a single sentence. It is addressed by one Arab Prince to another, and runs thus :—" In the Name of God, the Merciful, the Compassionate, We, 'Obeyd-ebn-Rasheed, salute you, O 'Abd-Allah, son of Feysulebn-Sa'ood : Peace be upon you, and the mercy of God and His blessings. . . . Now may God forbid that we should hear of any evil having befallen you. We salute also your Father Feysul, and your brothers,

* I take this "letter" from Palgrave's "Central Arabia," in which charming book all the details to which I allude are given in full. See vol. i. chap. v. p. 209.

and all your family, and anxiously await your news in answer. Peace be with you." That surely is a very pious and Apostolic letter. Yet it was written by a prince whose innumerable treacheries and murders had earned him the surname of "the Wolf:" and the omitted sentence charged two innocent travellers, an Englishman and a Syrian, with a crime punishable by death in the country for which they were just starting. With a courtly smile, and as a recommendation to favour, he gave them this pious treacherous letter, in which death and murder lurked under devout forms, and which would certainly have cost them their lives had they delivered it.

It would not be wise to lay too much stress, then, on the mere retention of pious forms and phrases, or to sigh for a return to Apostolic methods of correspondence. What we really want is *the Apostolic spirit*,—that courteous, generous, devout temper which gave beauty and completeness to all Paul did and said. Apart from that, in what stead will forms of devotion, however perfect, stand us? Having that, we may, very safely, leave it to adopt or create its own forms. It is not the absence, whether from our letters or our lives, of gracious standing forms corresponding to the salutations and benedictions, the prayers and thanksgivings of St. Paul's Epistles to his friends, which we need to deplore; but the too frequent absence of that humble, devout, charitable spirit which should be ours if we are Christ's, and which, were it ours, would breathe through all our utterances and all our conduct. What we want is, not more leaves shaped after an antique ecclesiastical pattern, but more of that noble Christian life which brings forth ever new, and ever better, fruit.

II. "Christianity," said Mr. Canning, in one of the debates on the Emancipation of the West Indian Slaves, "grew up amidst the scenes of tyranny which are described in the sixth Satire of Juvenal. It recognized the institution of slavery. How can it be said to be essentially adverse to that institution?" The question is of no slight moment, and should be fairly met. Nevertheless, it is not easy to meet it fairly. Not at all, however, because

D

we have any doubt that the Gospel of Christ is
" adverse " to " the institution of Slavery," but because we know it to be *essentially* adverse, adverse,
that is, *in essence* and substance rather than in outward form.   For on this, as on so many other points,
the Gospel furnishes us with no definite maxim, no
portable and unalterable rule of conduct; but it lays
down a general principle as large and flexible as
human life, and leaves us to apply that principle to
the varying conditions of humanity, to the changing
needs of the changing moment.   Now to master
and apply general principles requires an insight, a
patience, a loyalty to truth which few men attain,
or will be at the trouble to use.   Unskilled and
impatient, they, for the most part, crave definite
sharply-cut precepts which will apply themselves.
They must always have a pilot aboard who will
relieve them of the labour of thought, the burden of
responsibility.   Give them only the chart and compass of general principles, and they feel themselves
cast upon a troubled sea, whose paths are all unknown
to them, and whose waves cast up only mire and
dirt.   Nay more, they cannot see their brethren,

however patient and skilled, embark on this wide tossing sea, without instantly foreboding disaster and wreck. It is very much, I apprehend, because the Gospel lays down no sharp rigid rule on Slavery, and because men will not be at the pains to study those broad general principles which shade into all the conditions of human life, taking as well as giving colour, taking that they *may* give, that many excellent men have doubted whether the institution of Slavery is, or is not, essentially adverse to the Gospel of Christ. Let us understand, then, that if we would know " the mind of Christ" on this question, we are not to expect any definite authoritative maxim addressed to the social conditions of His time ; but a general principle, applicable to all times and conditions, which we shall not discover without some research, or master without some pains.

But though the Gospel only gives us a principle of this kind, we may see it at work, in the churches of Ephesus and Colossæ for instance, and rapidly producing a social revolution deeper and broader than was ever yet effected by mere rule or authority. Nay, in St. Paul's letter to Philemon, we have a vivid and living picture illustrative of the action of this principle, a picture in which we see it carried to its last and fair result. It is in its handling of ˙Slavery indeed, that the interest of this Letter centres and culminates. Here the general principle is not only stated, but applied ; and in studying its application we shall gain our truest and deepest conception of the principle itself.

What, then, was the condition of the slave in classical times ? and how did the Gospel apply itself to that condition ?

The slaves of classical antiquity were a class of men degraded not only beyond any instance but almost beyond the comprehension of modern times. They were in the power of their masters even to the severest form of death, nay, even to those unnameable insults sooner than submit to which any man worthy of the name would be " blithe to find the grave." They could own no property, nor hold any sacred domestic relationship. Their time, their faculties, their very persons, were not their own. They had no standing in any legal court, and were never examined except under torture. They were

---

beat and buffeted in wanton cruelty, or caressed to their dishonour: Epictetus, the Stoic philosopher,* for instance—who, like Onesimus, was a Phrygian slave, and like him, was now in the precincts of Nero's palace—had his leg broken by his master, who, for mere sport, began wrenching it this way and that. They were often compelled to fight with wild beasts in the arena, or were murdered by the gladiators to make a Roman holiday.† If they multiplied too rapidly, they were reduced by wholesale exter-

---

* Epictetus, born at Hierapolis in Phrygia, was, say *A. Gellius* and *Suidas*, slave to Epaphroditus, a freedman of the Emperor Nero, and the captain of his guard. Probably he was but a lad when Paul dwelt in his "hired house," awaiting Nero's caprice. Epictetus was the most Christian of the Stoic philosophers. Many of his sentences read as though they had been taken from our Lord's Sermon on the Mount, or from the Epistles of St. Paul. And I have sometimes thought that, while he was running about the Prætorium, he may have met his countryman, Onesimus, have been drawn by him into the hut of the Apostle, and heard so much of the truth as it is in Jesus as gave a tone to his subsequent meditations.

The anecdote referred to in the text we owe to Origen (Orig. cont. Cels. lib. vii.). As he tells it, it is an almost incredible instance of patient stoicism. According to the admiring Father, Epaphroditus one day took to violently wrenching his slave's leg about in frolic. Epictetus, without any appearance of passion, said to him with a smile, "If you go on, sir, you will break my leg." What he foresaw came to pass. And then, in the same quiet tone, he added, "Did I not tell you, sir, that you would break my leg?" The philosophic slave halted to his tomb. Long before his death, however, he became a freedman, and taught his pure lofty tenets to a large and noble audience.

† "Whenever the Roman entered his dwelling, the slave chained in the doorway, the thongs hanging from the stairs, the marks of the iron and the cord on the face of his domestics, all impressed him with the feeling

minations, and even in the noblest and most heroic states of Greece, it was reckoned an evening's pastime for the free youth to thin their numbers by an indiscriminate and bloody onslaught. Cato the Censor, held to be the most just and honourable of the Romans, habitually turned out slaves, who had grown old and feeble in his service, to die in the street, or suffered them to starve outright beneath his roof. And in this most miserable class there were many who were not " to the manner born;" men of noble lineage and learned culture, women reared in the tender seclusion of refined luxurious homes: and these, of all " the most deject and wretched" taken captive in war, lay at the mercy of men who knew no mercy for slaves, and were compelled to minister to their brutal lusts, or were tortured to death to glut their caprice.

that he was a despot himself; for despot and master were only other words for the same fearful thing, the irresponsible owner of a horde of human chattels. When he seated himself in the circus, and beheld the combats of men with beasts, or of men with their fellow-men, when he smelt the reeking fumes of blood which saffron odours could not allay, heard the groans of the wounded, and, appealed to with the last look of despair, gave recklessly the sign for slaughter, he could not but be conscious of the same glow of pleasurable excitement at the sight of death and torture which is ascribed to the most ferocious of tyrants.—Merivale's " History of the Roman Empire," vol. vi. chap. liv. p. 399.

With these unhappy creatures St. Paul, as he travelled from city to city, was constantly brought into contact. And to a man of so humane and generous a temper, his quick sensibility and burning indignation against injustice coming to the aid of the general Hebrew resentment against slavery,* their miserable estate must have caused many pangs. Nor was it only his personal and national sensibilities that were touched and offended, but also his zeal for Christ,

---

* It was a frequent habit among the Jews, as we learn from many passages in the Old Testament, to purchase slaves or servants. But we are not to suppose that the Hebrew servitude bore any resemblance to the slavery of Greece and Rome. Ginsburg, himself a Jew, and therefore speaking with some natural indignation, has a capital note on this point, in his "Coheleth," pp. 282—4. I subjoin an abstract of his argument. The Hebrews had no name for a slave, which implied that he was a mere *thing*, or chattel. עֶבֶד, the common Hebrew name for a slave or servant, means a *labourer*, and is often applied to the greatest prophets and kings: while the Greek δοῦλος, means *one who is bound or chained*, and the Latin *mancipium* means *captured goods* (I think Mr. Ginsburg will find that the root idea of *mancipium* is *that which is bought, property*, not *plunder*: this, however, does not affect his argument). These names fairly denote the characteristic differences between Hebrew and classical slavery. The Hebrew servant was acknowledged to be a man, in the image of God. He worked with his master, and with him kept the Sabbath and sacred festivals, which released him from labour nearly half his time. The law provided that he should be instructed in morals and religion. If he escaped from his master, he could not be delivered up to him by the inhabitants of the city in which he took refuge. His personal rights were protected by the law: if he lost the use of any limb or organ of the body, through the brutality of his master, he was immediately manumitted; if he was killed, his master was tried for murder. He might marry his master's daughter: *his* daughter often married his master's son. If he were an Israelite, he was still regarded as a citizen, and a *hireling*,—could acquire property, therefore, and purchase his freedom. If he did not purchase it, it was given him in

and for the welfare and honour of the Church. He
had so learned Christ as to hold every man his
brother, as that nothing human was alien to him.
He believed that there lay before every soul of man
possibilities of recovery, of redemption, of holiness;
that the most abject might become noble; the most
sinful, pure. How, then, could he endure to see
any whose nature Christ had shared, and for whose
redemption Christ had died, condemned to a condi-

the seventh year; and when he was enfranchised his master was enjoined
to "furnish him liberally out of the flock, and the barn, and the winepress,"
that he might make a hopeful start in life.

Contrast with this humane conception and treatment of the Hebrew
slave, the conception and treatment of the classical slave. Aristotle defines
him as "a living and working tool;" Plato describes him as a being who
had "nothing healthy in his soul," as of "a race in which men possessing
any intellect ought never to trust," as "not to be spoken to as a free
man." Homer sings—

> "Half their mind wide-seeing Jove has ta'en
> From men, whose doom has Slavery's day brought on."

If the classical slave escaped, no refuge was open to him, the master pur-
sued him wherever he pleased, and when he caught him, branded him,
often on the face, with a hot iron. He had no personal or legal rights;
his very life stood in the hazard of his master's whim. He was a mere
chattel, not a man, and might be flung aside the very moment he ceased
to be of use. Ginsburg gives his authorities for each of these statements,
and has, I think, conclusively proved that the classical slavery could only
inspire loathing and resentment in the Hebrew mind. Merivale, the his-
torian, is of the same mind with the learned commentator. "The social
relations (of the Jews) seem to have been unusually pure, those above all
of master and servant were natural and kindly. Slavery among the Jews
was so confined in its extent and so mild in practice, so guarded by law and
custom, as to become a real source of strength instead of weakness to the
commonwealth."—"Hist. Rom. Emp.," vol. vii. chap. lix. p. 190.

tion more foul, and wretched, and hopeless than that of the brutes? Above all, how could he bear to see those who were of like faith with him, who held, as he held, every man to be brother to Jesus and a son of God, guilty of this monstrous wrong, and retaining brethren in the abject conditions of slavery, in which virtue was well-nigh impossible? For *them* to do that, was to deny the fundamental truths of the Christian faith : it was to resist the impulses of that charity which is of all Christian graces the top and crown.

These feelings and convictions seem to have grown in force during the two years St. Paul dwelt at Rome. In the letters he wrote at this period—the Epistles to the Ephesians and the Colossians, as well as that to Philemon—he gives special prominence to the question of Slavery ;* and by his injunctions to both slaves and masters endeavours, at least, to alleviate the rigours of bondage. There was more than one reason why this subject should be much in his thoughts. One reason was this : We

---

* Ephesians vi. 5—9. Colossians iii. 22 to iv. 1. Both these Epistles were written during St. Paul's imprisonment at Rome.

learn from Tacitus,* that, in the very year of St.
Paul's arrival in Rome, there occurred a frightful illustration of the infamous and cruel injustice with which
slaves were treated in the metropolis of the world.
Pedanius Secundus, prefect of the city, was killed
by one of his slaves; and, in accordance with the
wicked law of the time, the whole body of them,
amounting to a vast multitude of men, women, and
children, were publicly tortured to death, although
innocent, and acknowledged to be innocent, of any
complicity in the crime for which they suffered.
An atrocity such as this could not fail to make a
profound impression on the mind of the Apostle, an
impression as painful as it was profound.   And
when, soon afterward, Onesimus told him *his* tale,
that impression would be deepened; it would grow
more painful and absorbing.   Onesimus devoted
himself to the service of the fettered Apostle, and
displayed natural capacities and graces of character
which won his heart. He loved him as his own
son.   Yet this man, so capable, so grateful, so

* Ann. xiv. 42—45.

eager to serve, was a slave; and had been so degraded by his abject condition that, in a moment of
temptation, he had embezzled his master's goods,
although, doubtless, that master, a Christian of fine
character and high standing, had been as considerate
and kind as a slaveowner could be.

With his keen far-reaching intellect, St. Paul
could not but see that there was something fatally
wrong in this social relation ; that, whatever leni-
tives and palliatives might be applied to it, it could
only, being itself an evil, bring forth evil fruit. Yet
how apply the only sovereign and complete remedy?
Slavery was an established institution of the time ;
it was interwoven with all the relations and interests
—domestic, civic, political—of society. To pluck
it suddenly out would be to imperil the whole fabric
—probably, to destroy it. To command every
master to manumit his slaves, and urge every slave
to strike a blow for freedom, would virtually be to
proclaim a servile war, which would breed new
horrors, and which must end either in embittering
the bitter condition of the slaves, or, should they
achieve an almost impossible victory, in the exter-

mination or bondage of their masters. Now St. Paul was of a statesmanlike sagacity as well as of an Apostolic fervour : and therefore he hated the wasteful " falsehood of extremes." In his public Epistles he endeavoured to mitigate the evil which as yet—and because it entangled in its embraces much that was good—it would not be safe to destroy. He urged masters to remember that *they* had " a Master in heaven," to treat their slaves "with justice and equity," to " spare threats," and to do them good. And he urged slaves to remember that they might " serve the Lord Christ " in serving their masters, and that if they did all things " as unto the Lord," they would rob even their servile condition of its deadly sting. In short, he taught the common *manhood* of slaves and masters, their common *brotherhood* in Him " in whom is neither bond nor free ;" and thus raised the Christian bondman from the deep degradation of the classical slavery to at least the level of the Hebrew servitude.

To young and ardent minds this may seem, as indeed it often has seemed, a timid and unworthy policy : for they cannot endure that the evils they denounce should be tolerated, even for an instant.* Their motto is, " Let justice be done though the heavens should fall !"   I can only remind them that were strict immediate justice done, the heavens *would* fall, and crush the earth which now they bless.   Happily for them and for us, He who sitteth on the circle of the heavens hath long patience.   He is very pitiful, and of a most tender mercy, or our shrift would be short, our doom intolerable.   And therefore, whatever we may think of it, it is often our duty and wisdom to let the evil and the good seed grow together, since we often cannot pluck up the one without uprooting the other ; and to leave the separation of the tares from the wheat in the hands

---

* Schiller, in a well-known passage, sets forth the contrast between the rash revolutionary humour of ardent all-assailing youth and the gradual tentative method of ripe experience and practised wisdom, under very happy figures :—

> The way of Order, though it lead through windings,
> Is the best.   Right forward goes the lightning,
> And the cannon-ball ; quick, by the nearest path,
> They come, op'ning with murderous crash their way,
> To blast and ruin !   My son, the quiet road
> Which men frequent, where peace and blessings travel,
> Follows the river's course, the valley's bendings ;
> Modest skirts the corn-field and the vineyard,
> Revering property's appointed bounds ;
> And leading safe, though slower, to the mark.
>
> *Wallenstein*, Art I., Scene 4.

of the Great Husbandman. This was the course St. Paul took, the duty he recognized. Hating the evil as hotly as we can hate it, he saw that he could not suddenly and forcibly root it out without doing even a greater mischief than that he was fain to destroy; and, therefore, he bade men keep under the evil growths as strictly as they could, since at present it would not be safe to extirpate them.

But, not content with this, he also set himself to plant and foster good growths, which might be very safely left to check their evil rivals. In his Epistles to the Ephesians and Colossians he affirmed the common manhood, and the common brotherhood, of slaves and masters in Christ Jesus; and these were principles which, as they grew and expanded, were sure to overtop and stifle the evil he deplored. And, in his Letter to Philemon, he repeats his argument in a new form and raised to a higher power. As he revolved the case of Onesimus, seeking how he might best assail an institution which already threatened both the purity and the peace of the Church, groping on all sides if haply he might find some axe to lay to the very root of the evil, he lit upon a weapon of heavenly temper and force. This was what was then called "the fellowship," a word whose meaning we have naturally forgotten, since we have lost so much of the spirit; but which, so soon as we understand it, we shall find to be simply the principles of a common humanity and a Christian brotherhood raised to their highest expression, and invested with an added sanctity.

In the primitive time, then, in the days that followed the first Christian Pentecost, that which seems to have struck the new converts as no less novel and original than "the teaching of the Apostles," was the sort of life which obtained among them and their adherents.* While the Lord Jesus was still with them, the Apostles had formed a moving household, going with Him whithersoever He went, dwelling where He dwelt, eating of one table with Him. So, too, the disciples outside the Apostolic circle appear to have regarded themselves as members of His family, and to have met His

* "They," *i. e.*, the Pentecostal converts, "stedfastly addicted themselves to the teaching of the Apostles, *and to the fellowship*, and to the breaking of the bread, and t the times of prayer."—Acts ii. 42.

immediate followers as brothers and sisters, not simply as fellow-citizens or fellow-worshippers. And when He went up on high, the little company of believers in Jerusalem " continued with one accord in one place," living together on pleasant equal terms as members of one family—a family whose ties were drawn very close by the bitter and general enmity to which they were exposed from without. This happy " fellowship " of kindred hearts was the spectacle which took, and held, the eyes of the three thousand converts. *They* were strangers out of every nation under heaven, separated from each other by diversities of race and habit and tongue. Though they were of one faith, —for they were all either Jews or proselytes—their faith was but a slack bond of union. The temple was a scene of strife between warring sects and factions. Galilean and Judean, Hellenist and Hebrew, Pharisee and Sadducee, Herodian, Sanhedrist, and Roman partisan wrangled among themselves and with each other. Every clique, every school, every faction, every race had its separate synagogue where they worshipped apart.

Is it any wonder that men whose very religion was a dispute, and whose most solemn acts of worship often broke into bloody frays, when they saw the little band of Christians, " of one heart and mind,'' meeting " with one accord in one place," were arrested by a spectacle so singular, attracted by a "fellowship" so pure and tender and harmonious? Here were "a hundred and twenty" men and women of different races, grades, cultures, living together not only in an unbroken concord of worship and affection, but in a holy enthusiasm of love which made each the servant of all, and forbad any one of them to say that aught of the things which he possessed was his own! With what an eager gladness would the strangers out of every nation addict themselves to such a fellowship as this, and find themselves welcomed into a family and possessed of a home quick with love and goodwill!

This, then, was "the fellowship," the warm, sacred "communion" of the primitive Church, which, with the cords of its strong tender humanity, drew the new converts to its bosom and inspired them with a spirit akin to its own.

E

What was the secret of it? It was the vivid
absorbing consciousness of a common life in Christ.
He had come to teach a new faith, and give a new
commandment,—the faith, a holy trust in the redeeming love of God, the Father of all men,—the
commandment, an injunction to love one another
on the ground of a common humanity, a common
redemption, a common brotherhood. He had
illustrated this faith by becoming the sacrifice of
our redemption. He had kept this commandment
by loving all men with a love which the many
waters of a Divine grief could not quench. His Spirit,
the Spirit of love and self-sacrifice, had descended
on those who followed Him, and " filled " them
with the grace which dwelt in Him. Like Him,
they trusted in God the universal Father: like Him,
they loved every man his brother. How could
they but love and serve each other when one life
beat in every breast, and in serving each other they
served Him from whom their life sprang? Compared
with this sacred unity, what was the national bond,
or even the family tie? If to have derived flesh
and blood from a common family source, or to have

common national interests, and habits, and aims, were much; how much more was it to have derived the life of the spirit from the Christ in whom their brethren lived, and to have all their eternal habits, and interests, and aims in common!

To this "fellowship," which, after all, and, as we have just seen, is but the highest and most sacred expression of our common humanity and common brotherhood, the Apostles perpetually appeal, when they would urge their disciples to advanced stages of thought and action. It takes many forms. It is "the fellowship of the body—of the blood—of the life—of the sufferings of Christ:" it is "the fellowship of the light—of the faith—of the Spirit—of the saints." But, always and everywhere, it implies the happy equal intercourse of redeemed men who have been gathered into one family, one household,—a household and family in which the least are greatest, and the strongest serve, and the most eminent are the most lowly.

Now it is to this "fellowship" that St. Paul appeals in his Letter to Philemon. The appeal lies at the basis of his whole argument, but more than once it comes to the surface and finds clear expression. Thus, in ver. 6, he prays that " *the fellowship* of" Philemon's " faith *may become effectual in the full knowledge of every good thing which is in us,*" to the glory of Christ Jesus. And the meaning of the prayer is, that the community of thought and feeling which already exists between them—*i. e.*, between Paul and Philemon — may first become " an energy," and find its appropriate expression in all good works, not remain a mere concord of thought and sentiment, but pass on into a holy activity ; and then, that this active community of Christian sentiment and opinion may become per- fect and complete, Philemon, advancing to the furthest limit Paul has reached—to " the full knowledge of every good thing which is in " the Apostle, that so, keeping step and pace the one with the other, they may both mind the same things and be moved by the same affections toward the same persons. This is the general meaning of the prayer ; but of course the Apostle had a particular application of it in his thoughts. Paul had learned to love Onesimus, whom, as yet, Philemon held in distrust and disfavour. Paul regarded him, not only as a slave, but as a brother beloved, very dear to him (ver. 16); while to Philemon he was not a brother, but only a slave. And what the Apostle really intends in his prayer is, that Philemon should learn to share his feeling for Onesimus. He is quite sure that his love for the repentant slave is a " good thing:" and, as Philemon shares so many other good things with him, he would have him share this also. Their " fellowship " covers much ; let it cover all. He longs to feel that their sympathy and communion are complete. The desire grows upon him as he writes. And in the 17th verse, he adds : " *If thou art in fellowship with me, welcome him (Onesimus) as myself*"— implying that their fellowship could hardly be genuine and sincere unless, at least on this matter, Philemon should think and sympathize with him. To St. Paul it appears that it will be nothing short of a breach in their communion if, while he regards Onesimus as a dear brother, Philemon regards him as a runaway and felonious slave.

Our poet Tennyson sings :—

> In Love, if Love be Love, if Love be ours,
> Faith and unfaith can ne'er be *equal* powers :
> Unfaith in aught is want of faith in all.
>
> It is the little rift within the lute,
> That by and by will make the music mute,
> And, ever widening, slowly silence all.

And I do not know that we can have a better illustration of the Apostle's feeling. To his fervent and excited heart it seems as though, if Philemon's fellowship with him is not complete, answering point to point through its whole compass and range, it is no true fellowship at all. He virtually says : " We agree in much. There are whole broad tracts of thought thrown open to us by the Gospel of Christ in which we are of one mind. We love God, and Christ, and the Church ; we make many sacrifices that we may serve them : but, though we have all this in common, could I suppose that we should differ in thought and affection about this poor slave, that you should fail to recognize a brother in him who is as my own child to me; *that*, though to many it might seem a very small thing, would be so fatal a breach in our communion as would well-nigh break my heart : it would be a discordant note which would swell till it overpowered all the harmony of our love : it would be ' the rift within the lute '—little at first, perhaps, but slowly widening till all its music were hushed."

In St. Paul's judgment, then—and in this matter he is a higher authority than even Mr. Canning—the institution of slavery was " essentially adverse " to the Gospel of Christ, since it was a fatal breach in the Christian fellowship. In his public Epistles, he might be content, and that for very good reasons, to give only counsels of prudence and mutual goodwill. He might advise slaves to patience, obedience, and that divine eye-service which would redeem them from the fear of man : he might advise masters to consideration, forbearance, gentleness, and a dutiful remembrance of *their* Master in heaven.* But in a private letter to Philemon and Onesimus, his personal friends, he

---

* I have sometimes thought that St. Paul may have habitually called himself " *a slave* of the Lord Jesus Christ," both to remind the slaves in the Church that their servile condition need not impair their true dignity and freedom, and to remind masters of the considerate kindness which even a slave might claim at their hands.

could more fully open his mind.   And to these he
says, in effect :—" The real question is, Are you
brothers in Christ ?   Is this Christian brotherhood
to be a real ' energy,' an effective power, or is it
not ?   Are we to talk of ' *the fellowship*,' yet not
to acknowledge each other as *fellows*, as equals,
before our common Lord ?   Is the communion of
the faith to cover only acts of public worship, or is
it to extend to all the relations, and intercourses, and
duties of life ?   What is this ' fellowship ' worth,
if you, Philemon, may regard as lawful what I
condemn as a sin against brotherhood ; if you may
whip, and brand, and torture him who is ' as my
own heart ' ?   What is this ' fellowship' worth,
if you, Philemon, may sit at one board with
Onesimus, eat of one loaf, drink of one cup, sing
one psalm, and say ' Amen ' to his prayer ; and
then rise from your common worship to make his
life bitter to him with toil and cruel bondage ? When
I come to you, and I hope shortly to be given to
your prayers, am I to find one brother using his
freedom to put the other brother in chains ?   Must
I and Archippus, your son, who by then will have

further instructed Onesimus in the heavenly hopes of the Gospel, rise from your hospitable table to comfort the poor slave who trembles under your displeasure? or are we all, you and I, Archippus and Onesimus, to be true brothers in Christ, comforting and serving each other in the Lord?"

Now it is very easy to say that St. Paul did not condemn slavery, and thus connived at vice when it was strong and popular: but *can* we say it when once we have followed out the argument of this Letter? He dared not, though he dare do whatever might become a man and an apostle, demand the instant enfranchisement of all who were held in slavery, lest a worse thing should come in its place. But though he did not press for its immediate abolition, or urge on a servile war, does he not teach a truth which ultimately, as soon indeed as it was understood, cut up slavery by the very roots? * Is it

* No candid reader of ecclesiastical history will either deny that even from the first the Gospel greatly ameliorated the condition of the slaves of Christian masters, or claim that its true bearing on this question was recognized by the Church for many centuries. Long after St. Paul had entered on his rest, Christians, and even the clergy, held their brethren and sisters in bondage. Yet manumission grew more common as the years passed;

not this doctrine of "the Christian fellowship," as expounded and enforced by him, which has, in these last days, proved itself the conqueror of slavery, and in all ages has been the strength of those who have stood up for the weak against the strong and for the poor against the oppressions of wealth?

It is because the Roman Church, with all its heresies, has held fast to " the fellowship," refusing to recognize distinctions of race and class in the Church, and holding all her capable sons eligible to any—even the highest—office or dignity: it is, at least in part, because of this, that she has survived so many assaults, and still wields so great a power in the earth. It is because, much as we pride ourselves on holding the primitive doctrine and maintaining the primitive order, *we* have so largely let this " fellowship " slip from our hands, that we are

and it is significant that in one of the earliest rescripts of Constantine, the first Christian emperor,—that which set apart the first day of the week for worship—it was provided that the only purpose for which the legal courts might be opened on Sunday was the manumission of slaves (Cod. Theodos. II. viii. 1). Subsequent edicts made it penal to steal infants for slaves—a common practice,—or to punish slaves to excess, or to torture them to death; though the rudeness of the times still permitted much that the Gospel condemns.

so weak and do so little to win men to our communion. *Communion!* Why, what communion is
there among us? Can we affirm that the sense of
Christian brotherhood is as strong in us as even the
ties of neighbourhood, or political party, or natural
kinship? How many of us feel an inward fire of
love for all who are one with us in Christ? How
many of us would do as much to serve even a member of the same church as we would to serve a
neighbour with whom we were intimate, or to
secure the election of a member of Parliament who
held our political views? Look around you.
"Mark them which cause divisions." How many
they are! On what slight grounds, on what slight
pretexts even, will they disturb the peace of the
Church! With what arrogance they judge and
condemn brethren who are at least as wise as they
are, and whose lives are at least as pure as theirs!
How much do they care for " the fellowship " when
once it is put in competition with their whims, their
prejudices, their preferences?

And yet they and we are loud in our complaints
that men are not won to the faith of Christ; that

even of those who are won many decline to join the
Christian fellowship ! Had we not better leave off
prating about " the fellowship " till we have something a little more like " fellowship " to show ?
When, like the early converts, we are with one
accord in one place : when those who are without,
as they peer wistfully through door and casement,
see a Christian family, whose members are all aglow
with love and goodwill, dwelling together in the
happiness of mutual service and self-sacrifice : when
we can make them feel that they will find *a home*
with us, a true home, a home more free and pure
and tender than they can find elsewhere : when the
kindly household warmth shines through all windows,
and streams guiding and inviting rays into the dark-
ness without : then, if the Divine promises be true,
and the Divine laws hold their course, there will be
a crowd of eager applicants for admission ; our
Father's house will be filled, and His bountiful table
furnished with guests.

To hasten which happy consummation, let us
each do what, and all, he can.

II.

ST. JOHN'S LETTER TO KYRIA.

THE SECOND EPISTLE OF ST. JOHN.

THE Presbyter to the elect Kyria, and to her children, whom I love in truth; and not I alone, but also all who know the truth,

2. For the sake of the truth which abideth in us, and will be with us for ever:

3. Grace, mercy, and peace shall be with us, from God the Father, and from Jesus Christ the Son of the Father, in truth and love.

4. I rejoiced greatly that I found certain of thy children walking in truth, as we received commandment from the Father.

5. And now I beseech thee, Kyria, not as writing thee a new commandment, but that which we had from the beginning, that we love one another.

6. And this is love, that we walk according to His commandments. The commandment is this,

---

Ver. 1. "*Kyria,*" which means "lady," and is the feminine of "*Kyrios,*" or "lord," was a common name of Christian women, even so early as the first century after our *Lord's* advent.

Ver. 6. "The commandment is *this,*" that is, is *love.*

even as ye heard from the beginning, that ye should walk in it :

7. Because many deceivers are gone forth into the world, even they who confess not the coming of Jesus Christ in the flesh. This is the deceiver, and the anti-Christ.

8. Look to yourselves, that ye lose not the things which we wrought, but receive a full reward.

9. Every one that goeth beyond, not abiding in the teaching of Christ, hath not God. He that abideth in this teaching, *he* hath both the Father and the Son.

10. If any one cometh to you and bringeth not this teaching, welcome him not into your house, nor bid him good speed ;

11. For he that biddeth him good speed partaketh in his evil deeds.

12. Having many things to write unto you, I have no mind to use paper and ink ;

13. But I hope to come to you, and speak mouth to mouth, that our joy may be complete.

14. The children of thine elect sister salute thee.

Ver. 9. "Every one that goeth beyond," *i. e.*, beyond the term and limit of Christ's teaching.

Ver. 12. "*Paper* and *ink.*" ὁ χάρτης is the Egyptian papyrus. This brief letter was written on paper, therefore, and not, like more public and important documents, on parchment or vellum. τὸ μέλαν is the ink commonly made of soot and water thickened with gum.

The private letters of public men have, as I have said, a very special interest for us, since they enable us to review—and, if need be, to correct—our conception of them ; to compare their private with their public attitude, their familiar with their more studied and formal utterances ; and to determine whether or not their lives had the harmony of sincerity and truth. We have already put St. Paul to the test, and have risen from our study of his Letter to Philemon with a profounder impression both of his singular and varied capacities, and of the moral unity and grandeur of his character. Let us now see how St. John will bear the same test.

With him the process is much more simple, the result never for a moment doubtful. As we compare this Private Letter to an intimate friend with the public " general " Epistle which immediately precedes it, we can have no hesitation in pronouncing that the same spirit breathes through both, and in both assumes the very same forms of thought and utterance. Not only does the scholar detect in this Letter grammatical constructions and terms of expression peculiar to the style of St. John ; but of

F

the thirteen verses which compose it, no less than eight are to be found in the earlier and larger Epistle.* And in both the Letter and the Epistle the main theme is the same—love, love based on truth, and keeping the commandment. Indeed, the concord both of thought and style is so complete, so obvious, that it would be a mere waste of time to enter on any proof of it. There is no need to prove that the sun is shining when the very moment you step into the air you feel its genial warmth.

Nor is there in the case of this Letter much scope for historical illustrations such as we found helpful to us in our study of St. Paul's Letter to Philemon. All we know of it is, that it was written when St. John was an old man; and that it was addressed to a Christian lady, the mother of many children, mainly with a view to prevent her from extending her hospitality to certain heretics who denied the Incarnation of Christ. So much we

* For characteristic construction see Dr. Davidson's " Introduction to the New Testament," vol. iii. p. 482. Mill (Prolegomena, sect. 153) is my authority for saying that eight verses of the Second are to be found in the First Epistle of John.

know : but, besides this, there is good reason for believing that the Letter was written in the city of Ephesus ;* St. John, according to a constant tradition, ending his days as bishop of the church in that city. It is tolerably certain too—the Letter itself seems to imply as much—that the sister of the lady to whom he wrote was also living with her children at Ephesus, for St. John adds their greetings to his own (v. 14); nor is it unlikely that some of the elect Lady's children, nephews of the Ephesian matron therefore, were engaged in the traffic of that busy thriving port, since the Apostle gladdens their mother's heart by telling her how, on ·a recent occasion,† he had met some of them, and was much rejoiced to find that they were walking in the truth (ver. 4).

But who the Lady to whom he wrote was, and where she lived, is beyond the reach of even pro-

* Ephesus stood about the middle of the western coast of the peninsula known to us as Asia Minor. Its harbour was of an elaborate construction, and was conveniently placed for traffic with all the neighbouring ports of the Levant. It was the terminus of four great roads, along which passed the mercantile caravans of the time. With a picturesque site, a fertile soil, and a healthy climate, it was one of the most thriving and prosperous cities, the commercial capital, indeed, of the province.

† This seems to be the force of the Greek tenses used in the fourth verse of this Letter.

bable conjecture; although from St. John's intimate acquaintance with her, from his intention of soon paying her another visit, and from the intercourse which seems to have been maintained between her family and her sister's, it would appear likely that she resided in one of the Asian cities not far from Ephesus.   Possibly, she was connected with one of the seven churches to which the ascended Lord sent Epistles by the hand of John.*   Her very name has been matter of debate, owing in part to the fact that the construction of the first verse in the Letter is peculiar and ambiguous ; and in part to the fact that the Greek proper names, like many of our English names, were also words in common use. Hence the opening words of the Letter have been rendered, " The Presbyter to the Lady Electa,"† " The Presbyter to the elect Kyria,"‡ and, as in

---

* Rev. ii. and iii.   At least Sardis and Smyrna were in constant communication with Ephesus ; one of the mountain roads which led from Ephesus passing through Sardis, and one of its coast roads terminating at Smyrna.

† Clement of Alexandria, in his *Adumbrationes*, writes, " Scripta vero est ad quandam Babyloniam Electam nomine : " " It was written to a certain Babylonian lady, named Electa."

‡ The " *Synopsis Sacræ Scripturæ*," once commonly but erroneously attributed to Athanasius, a valuable relic of antiquity, says of John, γράφει κυρίᾳ,—" he writes to Kyria." The Syriac version retains *Kyria* as a proper name.

our authorized version, "The Presbyter to the elect Lady." *Now*, however, grammarians are pretty well agreed that the Lady's name is given in this opening sentence; and that, if given, it must be Kyria,*—the word Kyria meaning "lady," but being also a proper name.

The lady Kyria, then, is a woman of some station, much given to hospitality, a beloved friend of the disciple whom Jesus loved. She has many children, some of whom are living with her in her own city, if not in her own house; while others are at Ephesus, where *they* have an aunt, *she* a sister. This sister is also a matron with children of her own, she and they being under the pastoral care of the Apostle John. From these he learns that certain heretics are about to visit Kyria, and claim her well-known hospitality. Hence this Letter, in which he privately forewarns her of the injurious views they held, and entreats her neither to entertain them in her house, nor wish them "good speed" when they leave it (vers. 9, 10).

---

* The grammatical reasons for this conclusion are given by Dr. Davidson and Dean Alford *in loco.*

This is all we know or can conjecture, all we can make this Letter tell us, of Kyria, of her character and conditions and relations, and of the purpose of the Apostle in writing to her, although, owing possibly to the infirmities of age and the pressure of many duties, he had " no mind to use paper and ink." Who would not like to know more? Who does not feel that the Letter would grow in interest and instructiveness were more told us of Kyria herself and the conditions of her life; or did history enable us to read more fully the thoughts which lie between the lines traced by the Apostle's hand? It is natural that we should crave a wider and more accurate knowledge; but are we to learn nothing from the fact that our craving is not gratified? May it not be well for us that we know no more? May we not learn a valuable lesson from our very ignorance? I think we may. In the very silence of Scripture and the early Ecclesiastical History there lies a lesson which touches us close home, and all the closer the less we live, or are likely to live, in the memory and on the tongues of men. Had Kyria and her children been persons of great mark, filling a large space in the public eye, we should have heard more of them. In all probability, they were simple inconspicuous folk, such as might be matched in any Christian church whether of this time or that. And yet, because they " walked in the truth " and " kept the commandment," John loved them, and "all who knew the truth " loved them (ver. 1); " grace, mercy, and peace " were with them, " from God the Father, and from Jesus Christ the Son of the Father " (ver. 3). *On the like terms, we may have the same reward.* " The end of the commandment is charity, out of a pure heart, and of a good conscience, and of a faith unfeigned." If we keep this commandment, if we suffer it to reach its " end" in us, *we* shall have the love of God, and of Christ, and of all who truly know the Father and the Son, however lowly our estate may be, and though the great restless world which roars around us take no note of us. We may not live in history, and yet may live in the very heart of Him of whose eternal will the whole human story is but a various and " passing show."

This is the lesson of the silence of this Letter, and of Church History concerning it ; and this lesson, if we but learn it, will be of more value to us than a complete acquaintance with every detail of Kyria's life and correspondence. But there are other and more direct lessons for us in St. John's Letter, and these also we must try to learn.

I. The Apostle opens his Letter by assuring Kyria of his unabated love for her and her children : but the assurance is somewhat singularly and significantly worded. He says, " Whom I love *in truth ;* and not I alone, but all who love *the truth ;* for the sake of *the truth*, which abideth in us, and shall be with us for ever " (vers. 1, 2). Is that threefold repetition of the word "truth" an idle repetition ? John affirms that he loves them ; but it is in the truth. Others love them no less than he ; but it is they who know the truth. And what he and they love them for, is not because of any natural charm, any winning grace of manner or character, which they possess, but because of the truth which abideth in them. Nay, as if this were not enough, he prays in the next verse (ver. 3), that "grace, mercy, and peace" may be with them " *in truth*," as well as " in love : " and in the next he declares his joy that he had found other of Kyria's children " walking in *the truth*." What is this truth on which he lays so studious and remarkable an emphasis, and why does he emphasize it? No doubt he lays stress upon " the truth " because he was about to warn his friend Kyria against those who were disseminating error. It is easy to answer that part of the question, but to define what " the truth " is, is by no means so easy. One thing, however, is obvious enough—viz., that St. John cannot possibly mean by " the truth " what many logicians and theologians mean by it. They maintain that truth consists of accurate statements and propositions about natural or spiritual facts; that to assent to these propositions or dogmas is to know and receive the truth ; that to reject these is to reject the truth. But that St. John could not have accepted their definition is very evident. For he speaks of "the truth which abideth in us : " and he could hardly mean by that, that a certain assent to certain dogmas or propositions dwelt in them. He speaks of loving the lady

Kyria " in the truth ; " and he could hardly mean by
that, that he loved her in the assent to certain accurate statements about God and man. He speaks of her
children as " walking in the truth ; " and he could
hardly mean by that, that they were walking in an intellectual assent to dogmatic propositions. What did
he mean by the truth, then ?   The full answer to that
question might lead us very far and deep.   But for
the present it will be enough to remind you, that to
St. John the Lord Jesus Christ was " the Truth "
—truth vital and incarnate.   Christ was the centre
of his system of thought, as He was of St. Paul's.
They both held that in Christ " dwelt all the
fulnesses of the Godhead," and, among these
fulnesses, all natural and human ideals, all that is
imperfectly expressed in Man and in the Universe ;
and that, therefore, He was the absolute eternal
Truth.   To St. John truth was not a notion of the
mind, or a set of notions, however large and accurate ;
it was no theory about God, but God Himself, and
God manifest in the flesh in order that we might
know Him and partake His life.   With him, to
" love in the truth " was to love in the Lord ; to

"walk in the truth" was to tread in the Lord's steps; to have "the truth abiding in" him was to have the Lord abiding in him, to have the very life and spirit of the Master on whose breast he had once lain. All knowledge, all wisdom, all life, all love, are, according to the Apostolic theology, from Christ, and in Christ; and because Christ dwells in him, he loves all in whom Christ dwells.

This was what St. John meant by "the truth:" what we also should mean. For it is not enough that we should have our theory, even though it should be of a scientific accuracy so far as it goes, about God and His relations to the world. We must have a vital personal relation to Him if we are to walk in the truth, and love in the truth, and have the truth abiding in us. We must feel that all true perception, all holy affection, all grace of character, are His gifts—gifts in which He communicates Himself to us. We must recognize these wherever we find them, whether in ourselves or in our brethren, not as proofs that we and they hold a certain creed about Him, but as signs which disclose the indwelling of His Spirit. We and they may hold

different, and in some respects adverse, creeds—that
is to say, our poor theories about God, which come
limping so far in the rear of truth, may differ and
contend : nevertheless, both they and we may hold
the very truth ; for God, whose action and grace
are not limited by our intellectual conceptions of
Him, may dwell in both. It is only as we recognize
the truth, not as an hypothesis, nor even as a science,
but as a living emanation and impulse from the very
heart of God in Christ, that we can be said, at least
in St. John's sense of the words, to walk and love in
the truth, to rest in the truth, and be assured that
the truth abideth in us and shall be with us for ever.

II. This, then, is the first cardinal point in the
Letter of St. John to Kyria—that Christ the Truth
must dwell in us, and be at once the motive, the
power, and the object of our love. The second
cardinal point is, that Love must be, or include,
Obedience. "This is love," writes the Apostle,
" that we walk according to His commandments ;"
and again, " *The* commandment—*i. e.*, the one
commandment which includes and fulfils all other

commandments, and which has been with us from the beginning and will be with us to the end—is "that we love one another." But has not the Apostle slipped unconsciously into a vicious circle of thought? First, he tells us that to love is to keep the commandments; and then, that to keep the commandments is to love: first, love is the law; and then, the law is love. Let us a little consider what he means.

Now remember that he is writing to a woman. And a woman, the more of " pure womanly " there was in her, would surely be the more apt to think of love as anything but a commandment, or as an obedience to a commandment, imposed upon her from without. She would be apt to say, "Love has nothing to do with law. It is not in the power of the will. It springs up unbidden in the heart. I do not love because I ought, but because I must. I cannot love because I am bid to love. I often love where, if my judgment were unbiassed by the partialities of passion, I should condemn." Whether or not this be the true conception of love, no one will deny that it is very generally entertained, at least by the sex which knows, or assumes to know, most of that gracious mystery. And it is not difficult to see how this view, strongly held, might degrade love into a mere taste, a mere sentiment, a mere preference. It is not difficult to see how the lady Kyria might come to think that her love had its origin in her own heart, and might be safely trusted for its continuance to her own strong tender impulses; how she might separate it from obedience, make it unpractical, reduce it to a mere play of emotion, and so deprive it of all the sacred and severe loveliness of Duty. If passion is to acknowledge no law, to have no noble controlling motive and inspiration; if it is to pour itself out at its own sweet will instead of flowing within the inviolable bounds of obligation, then its very strength is its peril, and that utter devotion to another which in itself is so beautiful is almost sure to be abused to its own hurt. And therefore it is, I suppose, that the Apostle repeats the word "commandment" as often as he repeats the words "truth" and "love:" these three being the master-words and key-words of his Letter. In effect he says to his friend, " You must not take your love for Him who is the Truth as the creature of your own instincts, or trust it to the strength of your own impulses. You must be on your guard lest it should degenerate into a mere sentiment or emotion. It is at once a commandment and an obedience to all the commandments. It is a grace; but a grace which is under law. You are *bound* to love Christ as well as drawn to love Him; it is your *duty* as well as your choice. And if you do love Him, passion will induce action, affection will induce obedience. Do not imagine that the new world of thought and feeling into which you have been introduced by the Gospel of Christ hangs in the air, that it has no basis in the past and no attachments to it; that the ancient Hebrew Law has passed away, and because we are under grace we are no longer under law. The whole Hebrew canon was but 'Love God and man' writ large. And therefore the new commandment of the Gospel is ' an old commandment which we have had from the beginning;' and to love is to keep the commandments. In their essence and substance, they are still in force, we are still bound by them; though now, if we are really moved by the love of Christ, our obedience will be voluntary and instinctive. On the one hand, therefore, cheerfully accept the restraints and supports which only the sense of duty will give to love; and on the other hand, remember that the commandment which controls your heart is the commandment of a Father, of a gracious and reconciled Father, *His* Father as well as yours, that so love may inspire and strengthen duty."

So far, therefore, from treading a vicious circle of thought, the wise Apostle sweeps a most wholesome and animating circle of thought. His constant antithesis between Law and Love is intended to teach that love must clothe itself in forms of obedience, and that obedience to law becomes perfect liberty when inspired by love. He marries Love to Duty, Duty to Love, and forbids us to put asunder those whom God has joined. Love, as mere passion, is very strong and urgent, but often reacts into even fatal languors. Duty, as mere obedience, is very constant, severe, authoritative; but often breeds

weariness and repugnance. But the two united—
Love and Duty, not opposed, but hand in hand—
are precisely helpmeets; they were "made for each
other," the one coming to the other's aid just where
and when it is most in need of help. A woman, for
instance, may love her husband passionately at first;
but if in her love there be no sacred sense of duty,
its force may soon be spent and dulled: she may
find, or fancy, that her affection meets no return, or
an insufficient return; and, solicited by the sem-
blance of a warmer devotion, may suffer her love
to wander from him to whom it is vowed and due.
Or a woman, mindful in part of her vows, may
obey her husband; but if love be not the motive and
strength of her duty, the duty will soon grow
irksome, intolerable even, should the spring of love
in her heart be touched by an alien hand. But the
true wife, she in whom love is an awful and sovereign duty, as well as a happy choice, and for whom
all duty is perfect freedom, because love is its inspiration and strength,—she is in no peril: if for
a little while love droops because it finds no return,
Duty steps in to comfort and aid it; if for a time

G

duty grows hard and irksome, Love steps in, and, lo, the yoke is easy and the burden light. And in like manner, the man whose devotion to Christ is to be true and perfect, needs both love and duty; or, rather, he needs love both as a passion and an obligation, that the one may have help and comfort of the other, according to God's holy ordinance. *We* need both. We need to think of Christ as our Friend and Saviour, of His eternal love for us, of all His grace and tenderness, of all He suffered for us and all He gives us, till a sacred impelling passion kindles in our hearts, a fervour of holy strength before which the bonds of sin and temptation will be as tow. We need also to think of Him as the Great God and Judge, of His claims on our service and obedience, of the constant inspection of His eye, of the balance in which He weighs and the book in which He records our deeds, and of the solemn assize to which He will call us, that the sense of duty may come to the aid of love when its force is somewhat spent. We cannot live always in a passionate rapture; nor will it be well for us to plod doggedly on beneath the yoke of law, never losing all sense of the yoke in the glad inspirations of a rapturous devotion. Love must now be its own law to us ; and, again, it must be a commandment imposed on us from without by a sacred and unquestionable authority, if our whole life is to be conformed to that of Christ. Like Him, we shall at times be driven on by holy ardours which constrain us to long for self-sacrifice, and to feel that we are straitened till our task be accomplished ; and at times, still like Him, we shall only be able to say, " If I may have my wish, let this cup pass from me : nevertheless, not as I will, but as Thou wilt." In short, love and duty must both be ours, till we rise into that happy world in which love and duty are one.

I have somewhere read of a brave unlettered Christian knight, who, when the priest was reading him the story of our Lord's crucifixion, smote his strong mailed hands together, and cried with a mighty oath, " Would God I had been there to strike but one right blow for Him !" *That,* no doubt, was the utterance of a true and intense passion. But you will readily understand that the good knight, despite the spring of love in his heart which answered to any skilful touch, might have a very slight and insufficient sense of Christian duty; that he might go from abbey or chapel to wage a deadly feud with a neighbour baron, to oppress his serfs, to be of an incontinent tongue, and of an unchaste violent life. And, on the other hand, I have often met men to whom Christ was a Master, not a Friend—a harsh and austere Master even; men whose service was prompted by fear and self-interest, not by love; to whom life shaped itself as a dreary succession of unwelcome tasks; and who never knew what it was to have their hearts spring up to God, as the lark springs into its native heaven, and pour itself out in the bright tender strains of an adoring praise. May we fall into neither mistake, but find duty ever prompt to control and reinforce our love, and love always at hand to inspire duty and transform it into a holy liberty!

III. But the duty which love demands will not

always be welcome to us. Love, because it is love and aims at our perfection, will sometimes require that we cross our natural tendencies and do that which it is very distasteful to us to do. The lady Kyria, for instance, was, as we infer from this Letter, given to hospitality. No doubt it was a pain to her to close her door against any member of " the household of faith " who asked for admission; and a special pain to close it against teachers, or even those who assumed to be teachers, of that Gospel to which she owed so much. Yet this is precisely what St. John bids her do. If any came to her who went beyond the teaching of Christ, any who aimed at a higher spirituality of view than that with which she was familiar, she must cross her native hospitable instinct, and refuse to receive them into her house. We may be very sure that St. John had some good reason for demanding this sacrifice—that he enjoined this unwelcome duty on Kyria, not because he wished to pain her, nor because he simply wished her to exercise herself in self-denial, nor because he would have men treated with discourtesy for a mere difference in theological opinion and speech.

It strikes one as singular, perhaps, that, of all the
Apostles, the Apostle of Love should be the most
stern and urgent against " the deceivers " who be-
guiled men from the simplicity that is in Christ. He
denounces them in the most impassioned language ;
he will keep no terms with them : the old " Son of
thunder " reappears in his unmeasured denunciations.* The fact strikes one as singular ; but it is
not difficult to account for it. It simply illustrates
the well-known law of our humanity, that those
who are dowered with " the love of loves " are also
dowered with " the hate of hates." The more a
man loves Christ, the more he must hate anti-
Christ. Where have you married men such parti-
sans as in your own wives ? If one has a fault to
find in you, it is best not to mention it in *their*
hearing. And why ? Simply because their very
love for you has for its opposite pole hatred for those
who set themselves, or are thought to set themselves,
against you. And, in like manner, if a man love
truth, he must hate error ; if he love men, he cannot

---

* In his First Epistle, for instance, he calls them "liars " (ii. 22) ;
" false prophets " (iv. 1) ; " anti-Christs " (iv. 3) ; and "children of the
devil " (iii. 7 and 10).

but hate those who mislead and injure them. The
Apostle John was "a *good* hater" in a double sense
—*i. e.*, his hatred was very profound, and it grew
out of his goodness. If the meekest of creatures
are ruffled into vehement anger when they suspect
harm to their brood, it is no wonder that the gentlest
and most loving of men, when he thought the honour
of his Divine Friend assailed and the safety of his
flock imperilled, flamed out in indignant commi-
nations.

The deceivers against whom he warned the elect
Kyria were men who were not content to "abide"
within the bounds of "the teaching of Christ;"
they would "go beyond" them (ver. 9). This is
all that the Apostle tells us of them, save that, in
another verse, he adds, that they did not "confess
the coming of Jesus Christ in the flesh" (ver. 7).
The description is not very definite. But it points
unmistakably to the Gnostic heresy, to refute the
growing power of which St. John is reputed to have
written his Gospel. Now Gnosticism, which drew
its origin from the mystic Cabala of the Jews, and

its chief nourishment from the Platonic philosophy, fell in with the whole set of thought in the Eastern world, where indeed it still lives in the Brahminism and Buddhism of India, China, and the adjacent regions. Its first rudiment or principle was the purity of the spirit, the impurity of matter, and the constant antagonism of these two. Matter was the root of all evil; spirit the source of all good. Asceticism and celibacy were easy inferences from this principle. He was the holiest of men who refused himself physical indulgence of every kind, who lived at the furthest remove from human passion, who had withdrawn from intercourse with his kind, and who, thus preserving the purity of his immaculate spirit, became absorbed in the silent and ecstatic contemplation of the Divine Perfections. Gnosticism took many forms, modulated through many variations; but this fundamental principle was never absent from it. And in the Church, among those who had received the Gospel of Christ, it became, as might have been expected from its close affinities with the Gospel, a very potent and widespread influence. As might also have been expected, it found much in the Gospel which it could not adopt, or could adopt only in modified and etherialized forms. All references to our Lord as having come "eating and drinking," all His comparisons of the kingdom of heaven to vineyards and feasts, were specially distasteful to the Christian Gnostics; they holding all that side of life to be noxious and unclean. But what most troubled them was the Incarnation of our Lord. The mere thought that the Divine Spirit should enter into a material body, become the subject of base human appetites and passions, and suffer the brutal handling of the Cross, was simply intolerable to them, incredible. And, therefore, in many subtle ways they evaded the plain force of the Gospel story. They maintained, for instance, that the Divine Spirit which dwelt in Christ was not " very God;" that it was only one of many emanations from the central ineffable Deity; that even this Divine Emanation only descended upon Him at His baptism, and departed from Him before He surrendered Himself to His enemies.

This was the current Gnostic view of human

life, and of that Divine Life by which humanity was redeemed to God. We cannot be far wrong, therefore, in assuming that this was the direction in which "the deceivers" of St. John's Letter "went beyond the teaching of Christ." In all probability, they maintained that the vile body, as the source of all our ills, must be rigorously kept under, all its appetites and passions denied even their innocent use and enjoyment; and that, because the flesh was vile and the irreconcilable antagonist of the spirit, Christ had not in any true sense taken a human body, had shared neither our birth nor our death. In short, and for the common Gnostic reasons, they denied, as St. John reminds us, "the coming of Jesus Christ *in the flesh.*"

But think what that denial involved ! If the Son of the Father has not come in the flesh, was not born, as we are, of a human mother, did not really assume our nature; then, because He is not one of us, His redeeming act does not touch us; at the best He is only an example of what we should be. Then, too, that sense of a common brotherhood which we have caught from Him is lost to us : we

can no more say, " All we are brethren, since He is
the Brother of each." If Jesus Christ did not
come in the flesh, the crucifixion of the flesh was
not the crucifixion of Christ. *He* has offered
no sacrifice, made no atonement on our behalf:
we have no Mediator with God; "there is no
Arbiter between us, to lay His hand on us both."
If Jesus Christ did not come in the flesh, He
did not ascend into heaven as our herald and repre-
sentative : it was no Man that went up on high,
only some thin abstraction whose assumption into
the eternal glory affords no proof that we also shall
rise and live. *The cardinal facts and truths of the
Gospel,* therefore, were denied by these " deceivers;"
they confessed not but denied the Incarnation, the
Crucifixion, the Ascension of our Lord, with all the
truths and hopes which, in our belief, rest on these
sacred facts. Is it any wonder that St. John—who
had " companied with Christ from the beginning,"
who had sat at His table, lain on His breast, watched
by His cross, stood by His open grave, gazed on the
beloved receding Form till the heavens received it
out of his sight, and who knew that these facts were

the only solid basis for the Christian faith and hope —denounced those who denied them as " the deceiver and the anti-Christ " ?   The Incarnation of Christ is the consecration of Humanity ; it makes us all brothers through our common brotherhood to Him.   The Crucifixion of Christ is the one sacrifice which taketh away the sin of the world, and assures us of the forgiving mercy of our Father in heaven. The Ascension of Christ is the triumphant demonstration and prophecy of human immortality.   To question these facts is to undermine the Christian Faith.   It is to annul the saving contents of the Gospel.   It is to transform the Rock of our Salvation into the baseless fabric of a dream.   Those who deny them were *anti-Christ*, and *are* anti-Christ.

And though John himself might meet them, and argue with them, and persuade them, it would not have been safe or well for many of his converts to listen to these " deceivers."   Because he loved those, he hated these, and would not have his friends " receive " them into their houses, or even wish them " good speed."   To wish them " good speed" in their destructive enterprise, was to become a partaker in it (v. 11), and in all the evils which resulted from it. Nay, it was even the worst wish one could frame for *them;* since so long as they sped in their evil task, they would not be likely to reconsider themselves and it.

But why does the Apostle warn *Kyria* against these men and their doctrine? Was there any special danger for her in a scheme of thought which seems to us, on its theoretical side, so fine-spun and fanciful, and, on its practical side, so austere and repellant? Probably, there was. That denunciation of the flesh as the root of all evil is a dogma which has always had charms for some of the noblest and most spiritual minds. Sad and bitter experience has taught them that most of the evils which afflict humanity do spring from the common abuse of the passions and appetites which have their seat or their organs in the flesh; and that to use these fleshly passions as not abusing them is a very difficult and perilous task. It has often seemed to them that it would be easier, perhaps also better, by one painful wrench decisively to break away from the world, to enter on a life of austere abstinence and self-mortification, than to carry on that conflict with the world and the flesh in which they have so often suffered defeat. And to the unselfish womanly nature, with its more sensitive and spiritual fibre, this course has often seemed the best and highest open to it. Many a noble woman, bent on maintaining purity of spirit and freedom from the baser cares and pleasures of life, has thought to gain her end by mortification of the body, by renunciation of the world, by sacrificing natural affection and forsaking domestic duties; and has sunk from a happy wife and mother into a hysteric devotee or nun. To be of the select few wholly devoted to God and great aims—this is an ambition which appeals to that which is sweetest and purest in the womanly heart.

It is an ambition which a great multitude endeavoured to realize in the early age of the Church. *Then*, for many reasons, it had a special power and charm, but mainly for these two. First, the Gospel was still new and wonderful, and raised the hearts of those who received it into a rapture of devotion which, in these later colder times, we can but faintly apprehend. The sacrifice of worldly goods and position was taken cheerfully : martyrdom was courted, and many of the primitive bishops had to rebuke the prevalent impatience to quit the world which the Christian should live to bless. Till heaven were won, how could time and energy be more happily expended than in brooding over the coming splendour, and in preparing for it by withdrawing from the petty cares and unstable delights of earth ? But if enthusiasm were one motive which lent force to the claims of an ascetic lowly life, another motive lay in the appalling, the incredible corruptions of the time. It is impossible so much as to name the vices which ran through the whole fabric of Greek and Roman and Asiatic society. There is no vile haunt in the wickedest capital of Europe, no circle of bullies and harlots in which a man would dare to suggest the criminal indulgences and subtle brutalities which were allowed and practised by the patricians, the poets, the philosophers, the priests of that time, as well as by its plebs and gladiators, its profligates and courtesans. And many a woman, her heart quickened by the Gospel to a new sense of purity, felt that there was no security, no peace for her, unless she could withdraw from the foul atmosphere which, so long as she remained in the world, she must breathe. No one at all familiar with the authors of that age, no one even who has weighed the meaning of the damnatory indictment which St. Paul lodges against it in his Epistle to the Romans,* can feel any surprise at learning that multitudes of the holiest men and women retired to the desert, or secluded themselves in cell and *laura*, to live an austere self-chastening life, and left the mad wicked world to reel after its lusts.

Kyria may have been very susceptible to the charm of the Gnostic doctrine and practice. A good, pure woman could hardly fail to be deeply sensible of it. Religious enthusiasm may have combined with the moral recoil from social corruptions to dispose her to abandon an abandoned world, to renounce the duties of the home for the pure austerity of the cell. And we can hardly have a

* Rom. i. 24—32.

stronger proof of the profound antagonism of the Gospel to an ascetic celibate life than the fact that in such a time St. John corrects her tendencies to it, or warns her against cherishing them. In this Letter his verdict, on a question on which the Church has been divided from his day to ours, rings out clear and loud. Whatever the corruptions of the age, whatever its social perils, St. John believed that it was better for a woman to be a matron occupied with household cares, and helping to keep the world about her sweet and pure, than to be a religious recluse occupied only in saving her soul out of the large merciful hands of God. "As kindly help to man," sings Schiller,* and it would seem that St. John was wholly of his mind,

> " As kindly help to man
> Was woman born ; and in obeying Nature
> She best obeys and reverences Heaven."

It was because the Apostle deemed Kyria's useful domestic life as the hospitable mistress of a large household, the tender gracious mother of many children, more consonant with the will of the Father

* " Maid of Orleans," Act iii. Scene 4.

H

and of the Son of the Father, than a solitary and
recluse life ; perhaps, also, because he knew her to
be very open to the temptations of spiritual enthusiasm, that he was urgent with her to deny her
hospitable instincts, and close her door against " the
deceivers " who were abroad.

And did not John rightly interpret the will o;
God and of Christ ?   Has *God* ever abandoned the
world, even in its corruptest age, that those who
serve God should be forward to abandon it ?   In
the very age in which Gnosticism achieved its
greatest triumphs, the Perfect Man did not seclude
Himself in cloister or cell, but went about doing
good, reclaiming harlots and bringing publicans to a
better mind.   *He* came, not fasting and abstaining,
but eating and drinking ; no austere eremite of the
woods, but a denizen of towns and cities, living
amid a widening circle of friends and with holy
women who ministered unto Him.   So far from
favouring asceticism, He first " manifested forth
His glory " at a marriage-feast.

Wedding mirth is holy mirth, then ; and church
bells are just as sacred when they peal merrily as

when they summon us to worship or toll over the open grave. We may "eat and drink to the glory of God" the Father. We may "dance and be merry" to the glory of the Son of the Father. We may "use the world as not abusing it." The self-renunciation which Christ demands of us is not a painful abstinence from natural appetites and delights, but that wise use of them, that temperate and thankful enjoyment of them, which will do both us and others good : it is the expulsion of the selfishness into which we so easily sink by that divine charity which is bent on serving its neighbours, and which then serves itself best, and enters into its true happiness, when it can most effectually serve them. And therefore the workshop or the home may be more holy than the desert or the convent. Therefore the bridegroom who chooses his wife and orders his ways in the fear of God, is a better, as well as a wiser, man than the monk who denies himself a present happiness that he may escape a future misery. Therefore the bride, standing with lifted foot before the threshold of a new home and a new life, her heart moved by the tender ambition of winning love by showing love, and doing good by being good; or the mother ruling children and servants by force of love, and making their life sweet to them by a thousand graceful kindnesses, is fairer and holier in the sight of Heaven than the pale shorn nun who devotes her days to morbid introspection and hysterical spiritual excitements, or than even the sister of mercy who chooses her own work instead of letting God choose it for her.

But to return to our Letter. St. John forbids Kyria to receive the Gnostic heretics, who went beyond and against the teaching of Christ. What are we to learn from that? That *we* are to sit in judgment on men, to pronounce this man a heretic, and that a deceiver; to refuse to receive them into our house, or so much as bid them " good speed " when, hurt and neglected, they turn from our door? I think that is not quite the lesson we should learn. If, indeed, men thrust themselves upon us who will not " confess that Jesus Christ is come in the flesh," who deny, therefore, the cardinal facts and truths of the Gospel of our redemption, we cannot of course wish them to speed in the work of their denial, since that would be to share their sin. But before we refuse any brother, or professed brother, a hospitable welcome, let us at least be sure that he does deny the Incarnation of Christ : for many have been condemned, not because they were guilty, but because their judges were hasty or ignorant; not because there was any obvious mote even in their eye, but because the beam in the eye of their judges cast a dangerous shadow on that of those whom they had summoned to their bar.

Let us also reflect on these two facts :—First, that St. John did not turn " the deceivers " out of his own house, but simply advised Kyria not to admit them to hers ; and, secondly, that St. John was in a small and despised minority, while those who denied Christ were in a large prosperous majority.

The first fact, the fact that St. John is advising Kyria's course of action, not announcing his own, should remind us, I think, that persons of different calibre and culture have, or may have, different duties. For me to receive a man who calls in question the fundamental articles of the Faith may be wrong and dangerous while my faith is weak; since in that case I am likely both to get harm and to do no good. But if you are strong, wise, immovable in the faith of Christ, your duty may be the very opposite of mine. It may be your duty to receive him, to argue with him, to give him of your light, and to win upon him by your kindness. For many a man is confirmed in a heresy, from which, had he been kindly and wisely met, he would soon have been set free, simply by the foolish outcries, the ungracious carriage, the unjust denunciations of those who regard themselves as the very pillars of orthodoxy. And we should care more to win a brother than to build up our reputation on the ruins of his.

The second fact, the fact that when he gave this advice to Kyria, St. John stood in a small minority, may well suggest the question, whether our whole duty to the heretic and misbeliever may not have changed with our changed circumstances. It is not

altogether . incredible that if St. John and the lady
Kyria were alive now—*i.e.*, upon earth, for of
course they are very happy together in heaven—he
would give her quite another counsel. *Then*, when
the Church was a comparatively small community,
with but few wise or noble members ; when Christians like Kyria had only fragments of the New
Testament in their hands, and could only hope for
an occasional visit from a teacher fully instructed in
the mind of Christ ; when their pastor might chance
to be " a lover of pre-eminence " and " a prater of
malicious words," like Diotrophes ; and when they
were exposed not only to the frightful corruptions of
the time, but also to the insidious advance of " deceivers," who, under cover of an exalted spirituality,
undermined the Gospel of the Cross, and affirmed
that the only safety lay in instant flight from an evil
world : there were perils in such visits as that pro-
posed to Kyria which could not possibly attend
them now. *Now*, when misbelievers are comparatively few, and the whole set of the time is against
them : when the wise and noble of the land, if
not " for " Christ, are not " against " Him : when

the current morality of our vilest classes is in some respects higher than that of the virtuous Roman or Greek : and when the Church, sunk in sloth and routine, is wofully apt to mistake a wise man for a fool and a teacher of primitive truths for a schismatic:—I doubt whether even St. John himself might not say, " By all means show these poor men what kindness you can, and try to win them to a better mind.   They are not likely to unsettle your faith, and if they do, you can easily get whatever help you need."

But, after all, the best lesson we can learn from the Apostolic counsel to Kyria is this :—That, if we would keep our love for Christ the Truth intact, we must often do that which we do not like to do. Hospitable Kyria could hardly have *liked* to turn even anti-Christ himself from her open door ; yet it is just this which John requires of her.   And we may not like to deny ourselves in our ruling bent— to show a cordial kindness, for instance, to reputed heretics, or to make a stand for unpopular truths, or to waive our clear rights that we may win a brother's love : yet even this may be demanded of us. For the truth is that as yet we are not redeemed, but are only being redeemed, to a whole-hearted service of God. To put Him first and His righteousness, and to keep them first, is not easy to us, but very hard. *Christ* did it : but if we would follow Him " whithersoever He goeth," we must take up our cross : there is no true following of Him without that. And often we think more of the sharpness, or the weight, of the cross than of the delight of following Him. Let us try—ah, let us try—to remember that we are following Him, following Him to the glorious high throne of an universal service ; and then even the heaviest cross will grow light, and the sharpest yoke easy, and, though bearing both, we shall nevertheless find rest to our souls.

III.

ST. JOHN'S LETTER TO CAIUS.

THE THIRD EPISTLE OF ST. JOHN.

THE Presbyter to the beloved Caius, whom I love in truth.

2. Beloved, I pray that above all things thou mayest prosper and be in health, even as thy soul prospereth.

3. For I rejoiced greatly when brethren came and bore witness to thy truth, even as thou walkest in truth.

4. Greater joy have I none than this, to hear that my children are walking in the truth.

5. Beloved, thou provest thy faith in whatsoever thou doest for the brethren, especially when they are strangers ;

6. And these have borne witness to thy love before the Church : whom thou wilt do well to forward on their way after a godly sort ;

7. For they went forth on behalf of THE NAME, taking nothing of the Gentiles.

8. *We*, therefore, ought to support such persons,

Ver. 2. *Above all things*, or " *in* all things."

Ver. 5. *Thou provest thy faith.* Literally, " thou doest, or actest, faith:" *i.e.*, you act it out, put it into an appropriate deed.

Ver. 6. *After a godly sort.* Literally, " worthily of God:" *i.e.*, in a manner due to the servants of Him in whose service both thou and they are enrolled.

---

that we may become fellow-workers with them for the truth.

9. I wrote somewhat to the Church (on this point); but that lover of pre-eminence among them, Diotrophes, receiveth us not.

10. Wherefore, if I should come, I will bring his deeds to mind; his prating against us with malicious words : and how, not content with that, he neither receiveth the brethren himself, nor suffers those who would, but casteth them out of the Church.

11. Beloved, follow not that which is evil, but that which is good. He that doeth good is of God ; he that doeth evil hath not seen God.

12. To Demetrius, testimony hath been borne by all, and by the truth itself : yea, we also bear testimony (to him), and ye know that our testimony is true.

13. I had many things to write to thee, but I have no mind to use ink and reed,

14. And I hope very shortly to see thee, and speak with thee mouth to mouth.

15. Peace be with thee. The friends salute thee. Salute the friends by name.

Ver. 13. *Reed.* ὁ κάλαμος, the writing-reed. This, says Lücke, with the paper and ink mentioned in 2 John 12, were the writing materials of the New Testament.

In writing to the elect Kyria, the Apostle John incidentally sets before us his conception of the duties of a Christian lady : in writing to the beloved Caius, he shows us what he conceived to be the duties of a Christian gentleman. The lady Kyria does well in that she rules her household, loves her husband, and wisely trains her children in the love and practice of the truth. As a busy hospitable matron she is nearer God than she would be were she to despise the flesh, with its appetites, duties, relationships, and aspire to become a creature much too bright and good for human nature's daily food. And, therefore, she is not to listen to, or entertain, or even succour with friendly wishes, the heretics who deny that Jesus Christ is come in the flesh; who hold the flesh in abhorrence as the root of all evil, and urge silly women to renounce their natural functions for an austere and recluse life. This, in brief, is St. John's conception of what a Christian woman should be, of her place and duty in the world. His conception of what a Christian man and gentleman should be, both in the world and in the church, will disclose itself to us, I hope, as we study his Letter to Caius.

We have only the slightest materials out of which to put together an historical framework for this Letter; and even these are in part conjectural. When it was written, *St. John* was bishop of the church at Ephesus; an old man now, to whom the use of paper and pen, ink and reed, was irksome: whose sentences, when he writes, are therefore very curt, though he still loves to expatiate, as old men will, in conversation with his friends, and to speak with them " mouth to mouth." We know absolutely nothing, except what we learn from St. John, of the three men mentioned in this Letter,—Demetrius, Diotrophes, and Caius, although Ecclesiastical Tradition, with its usual munificence, raises them all to the episcopal bench. Probably, however, " beloved *Caius*" was a layman, a convert of St. John's,* since the Apostle ranks

---

* " He was probably a convert of St. John (v. 4), and a layman of wealth and distinction in some city near Ephesus."—*Smith's* " *Dictionary of the Bible.*" *Art.* " *Epistle of St. John.*"

him among his " children," [and a member of an
Asian church in the vicinity of Ephesus. Tradition
connects him with that of Pergamos, of which
church it is supposed that that " prating lover of pre-
eminence " (vers. 9, 10)—what an epithet for a
Christian Apostle to have to fling at a Christian
pastor !—Diotrophes was presbyter. From the
Letter itself we may infer that Caius was a man of
good position and generous temper, since he both
had, and used, the means of hospitality, receiving
even "strangers," and strangers whom his own
pastor had denounced as heretics, if only he recognized them as " brethren " (vers. 5, 6). *Diotrophes*
appears to have been a vain, loud, specious priest,
with what the vulgar call " a great gift of the gab,"
who loved to *get* his own way as well as to have it ;
and who hated the messengers of the truth com-
mended to him by St. John, in part because they
were bent on carrying the Gospel to the *Gentiles*—
he himself being no doubt both a Jew and of the
Jewish faction ; and in part because they " took
nothing " in return for their services—a very dangerous example, which might suggest unwelcome

I

comparisons : in short, a masterful self-willed man who could not endure even the gentle yoke of a St. John, and was very ready to fulminate excommunications against any of his flock who did not think as he thought and do as he bade them (vers. 9, 10). What a happiness for us, my brethren, that that type of priest has been extinct— O these many hundred years !

The good *Demetrius*—to whom the truth itself, the Apostle, and all the brethren bore witness— seems to have been the leader of the little band who had devoted themselves to the service of the Gentiles. Him John had first sent to Pergamos (let us assume Pergamos to have been the city of Diotrophes and Caius) with a letter of recommendation to presbyter Diotrophes, only to find that neither would he receive them nor suffer them to be received by those who were willing to entertain them (vers. 12, 10, 9). *Now* the Apostle sends these devoted missionaries of the Cross to Caius the layman, in the hope that, as he had shown them love and goodwill when they were strangers (vers. 5, 6), now that he knows them for brethren, and brethren whose disinterested character and noble aim are attested by the Apostle himself, he will help them forward on their journey and support them in their work (vers. 6, 8). Such help, a kind generosity like that of God Himself, was their due; for these good men, who would take nothing of the heathen lest the heathen should misconstrue their motive, and confound them with the priests who cared very little for serving the altar so that they lived by it, had nothing, or very little, of their own; and were therefore compelled to depend on the love of brethren who knew how pure their motives were. Pastor Diotrophes, however, did not care to have strange teachers, who possibly saw through him and did not see much in him to admire, going about among his flock, staying a month with this friend and a month with that, pleading in every house the cause of the neglected Gentiles. And it must be admitted that for a man who loved to have the pre-eminence, and trusted for it to his tongue perhaps rather than his life, it must have been very trying to have as such close neighbours to his throne men of a more royal spirit than

himself, men whose motto was, " Deeds not
words."

If we compare this Letter to Caius with the
Letter to Kyria, we shall discover both correspondence and contrast between them. The
correspondence, both of form and of spirit, is indeed very close. The Apostle opens his Letter
to Kyria with an assurance of his unabated affection, and a prayer for her spiritual growth. He
is very glad to know that she and her children are
walking in the truth. He commends her love, and
urges her to love. He explains that the duty which
love demands is at times difficult and unwelcome,
and urges her to cross her natural hospitable bent
rather than receive those who are the enemies of the
truth. In like manner, St. John opens his Letter to
Caius with the assurance that he "loves" him
(ver. 1), and with a prayer that he may have a
sane mind in a sound body, and find all the outward
goods of life multiply upon his hands according to
his ability to use them for spiritual and noble ends
(ver.). 2 He is very glad to hear that Caius is

walking in the truth ; he has no greater joy than to hear that of any of his children (vers. 3, 4). He commends the love of Caius, as shown in receiving brethren who were strangers, not as strangers, but as brethren ; and urges him to exercise and prove his love yet further by helping Demetrius and his companions on their unselfish enterprise (vers. 5—8). And thus he incites him, for truth's sake and love's sake, to do a difficult and unwelcome duty ; for we can hardly suppose that Caius loved to· cross Diotrophes, to put himself in opposition to his pastor, and especially to a pastor so voluble, so petulant, so self-willed.

The correspondence between these two Letters is very obvious and complete then. Nor is the *contrast* less complete or less obvious. For the main purport of St. John's Letter to Kyria was to warn her against helping heretics or holding any fellowship with them. But the main purport of his Letter to Caius is to ask him to help certain reputed heretics, and to become a fellow-worker with them. And although, as we have seen, even the former Letter does not encourage us to sit in judgment on our

brethren and condemn them as schismatics ; nevertheless, it is matter for devout gratitude that, in His
gracious providence, God has put this latter Epistle
into our hands—an Epistle from which we learn
that men who differ from us may be in advance of
us, may have given more thought to the words of
Christ than we have, and found deeper and more
gracious meanings in them.   For if at times it be a
sacred duty to hold aloof from those who deny " the
coming of ·Jesus Christ in the flesh," and all the
saving facts and truths which that fact involves ; it
is often our most sacred duty to stand by those whom
Ignorance and Bigotry condemn as heretics simply
because their words breathe a larger than the current
wisdom, and their lives a more intense devotion.
Orthodox Diotrophes may have a loud tongue, a
great reputation, a quick eye and a keen scent for
his neighbours' errors, a prodigious power of damnatory objurgation, a lofty position in the ecclesiastical world ; and yet Demetrius, with his keen
insight into unrecognized truths, his ardent devotion
to neglected classes or lofty aims, and a disinterested
zeal which stands in rebuking contrast to our selfish-

ness, may be—nay, is—far the better man of the
two, although he has not a penny in his pocket, or
an anathema in his mouth, or a ready chorus of
public approval to back his words. The one may
be a selfish and prating lover of pre-eminence; while
to the other the very truth itself bears witness.
Should we possess " all knowledge " and " understand all mysteries," yet if we " have not charity,"
we are but ,as " resounding brass and a clanging
cymbal," even though the whole ecclesiastical
world dance to our tune.

But now let us gather such hints as this Letter
yields us of St. John's conception of the Christian
man and gentleman. The first point we have to
mark is, That the rudiments of character are the same
in the Christian lady and the Christian gentleman.
To Caius, as to Kyria, St. John insists on " truth "
and " love " as the only foundations on which
Christian character can rise. By the truth, as we
have seen, the Apostle means Him who is the
Truth. To love the truth is to love the Lord
Jesus : to walk in the truth is to tread in His steps.

And nothing lies closer to the heart of St. John, nothing gives him a profounder joy, than that his " children " should love the truth and walk in it. To have a reputation for knowledge, or eloquence, or faith, or charity, is not enough. The main question is, Are they true ? Does Christ dwell in them ? If He does, their graces have a living eternal root, and will continue to breathe their sweet odours and bear their precious fruit. If He does not, these graces have no living eternal root, let them spring from what they may ; and therefore they must soon fade, and fall, and die. Our very love must grow out of the truth. It must not be simply an emotion, or a passion, however intense. It must be based on a sense of duty, in order that when the fervours of passion cool, love may still be the regnant power. And therefore the Christian gentleman is one who walks in the truth, and labours for the truth. His whole life is shaped and ruled by the Spirit of Christ. His good works are done for Christ's sake, and not that they may be seen of men, or that he may, in virtue of them, win pre-eminence. Hence he never tires of them, since Christ is served by every good

work, whether it succeed or fail, whether men ap-
prove it or disapprove. His love endureth all things,
even if it cannot hope all things ; for every act of
love expresses his dutiful affection for his Master
and Friend, and so long as He is served and pleased,
it does not much matter whether or not our love
win any grateful response from our brethren.

But, again : If a man have these rudiments of
holy Christian character, he will be very indepen-
dent of the opinions of the world, and not unduly
affected even by the opinions of the Church, or of
those who assume authority in the Church and
affect to speak in its name. He will think for
himself. He will be ready to listen to all who
speak for Christ ; he will respect them " according
to their several ability ; " he will gladly defer to
those who show a larger wisdom than his own and
breathe a more devout spirit : but he will call no
man "Master : " he will pin his faith to no man's
sleeve. Lady Kyria may do well to avoid heretical
teachers ; but Caius will hear both Demetrius and
Diotrophes, and get what good he can from each of
them. Diotrophes may be vain, noisy, forward ;

very ready to ban those whose knowledge is larger
and whose charity is purer than his own : he may
hate novelties in thought or action, and condemn
any who will not walk with him, or will advance at
a pace which carries them to the front : but, nevertheless, he may hold very sound views of the
simpler truths which are for all ages and all conditions ; or he may even have a singular and curious
erudition in whatever illustrates past phases of truth.
Demetrius may startle us by the novel forms in
which he utters old truths, or may act in a fashion
so original as to surprise us into easy blame : he may
affirm that some of our *credenda* are mere human
appendages to Divine Truth : he may convict us of
a woful ignorance of the Gospel in which we boast,
or of not making the sacrifices which even our
conception of the Gospel demands : but, nevertheless, the truth may bear him witness ; he may
be taught of God that he may teach us ; he may
have proved his sincerity by sacrifices greater than
any he asks of us.   And if we are Christian men
and gentlemen, we shall listen to both Demetrius
and Diotrophes without a thought of fear, though

the one be called a heretic and the other a bigot, and though neither of them win our full concord of assent. Because He who is the Truth dwells in us, we shall not fear to listen to any man who speaks of Christ: we shall be sure that the Truth within us will recognize whatever truth comes to us from without. Because as yet the Truth dwells in us only in part, and is in much thwarted by our sin and folly, we shall expect to meet new and larger views of truth as the years pass, and shall very gladly welcome any new truth that breaks out upon us from God's holy Word, through whatever lips it may come. Nothing is so pusillanimous, nothing so clearly betrays the low spiritual level to which we have declined, no proof can more fatally convict us of not possessing the Truth, or not trusting Him, than that we should fear to listen to any scientific or critical exposition which clashes with our views, or is supposed to clash with them. With what face can we claim to be walking in the truth while our mind misgives us that, did we know a little more than we do, or hear all that men have to say, we should be driven from our path?

Once more: If we are walking in the truth, we shall love *all* who speak or serve the truth, even though a vain misguided Diotrophes should hate them. Strangers came to layman Caius when turned from his pastor's door, and in these strangers he recognized brethren: he loved them, or how should "they have borne witness to his love before the church"? and gave them what succour he could. And we must learn to find brethren in strangers. They may speak another tongue, hold other views, address themselves to a different task; but if the truth be in them and in us, the truth in us will recognize and respond to the truth in them: we shall prove our faith, clothe it in its appropriate deed, by according them our sympathy and aid. To some of us, perhaps Diotrophes himself may seem the greatest stranger of all, the most remote from our sympathies, because lacking in that charity which is the distinctive mark and feature of the household of faith. Even him, however, we must love, so long as we can find any truth in him, and any zeal for truth. If the Truth be in us, we shall love him even though he should cast us out of his

church without once suspecting that Christ's Church
may be larger than his.   We shall say, " ' He that
doeth good is of God; he that doeth evil hath not
seen God' (ver. 11): while he that doeth both
evil and good is, in so far as he doeth good, of God,
and in so far as he doeth evil, shows that he has not
seen God as he might and ought to have seen Him."
For it is very certain that many men are of God who
have never seen God as He is; and who are good
men, therefore, although their goodness be very
imperfect.   Nay, it may even be doubted whether
any of us have altogether seen God as He is.
Surely, we shall be better men than we are when,
awaking to see God, we are satisfied with His like-
ness !   Meantime, we are to acknowledge that all
good is of God, and that all evil comes of not seeing
God.   We are to acknowledge that even the little
good in a wicked man—and what man is more
wicked than a Christian pastor without charity ?—
is kept alive in him by the God who overcomes evil
with good ; and that the little or much evil which
mars the goodness of good men is owing to their
imperfect vision of the Perfect Goodness, and will

disappear as they rise to a clearer view of the
Divine Beauty and Holiness.

Honouring all truth, loving all that is lovely,
because the Truth is in us and the Love, we shall
very gladly " bring " one another " forward " on
the journey of life (ver. 6). This, indeed, is the
leading feature in the common, and not untrue,
ideal of a gentleman : he is courteous, and considerate, and helpful ; he postpones his own gratifi-
cation to that of others, finds his in theirs ; and
his chivalric instinct impels him to a very special
sympathy with the weak and the oppressed. This
is the duty which St. John urges on Caius. He
is to help and support his brethren, even when
they are strangers to him. And if they are few and
weak, while their opponents are many and strong ;
if humble self-denying Demetrius be wronged by a
vain, noisy, popular Diotrophes ; he is to be the
more prompt and earnest with sympathy, with
assistance. Let him, like a true knight, succour a
feeble and oppressed virtue. He may be very sure
that he shall not lack his guerdon, and such a
guerdon as will be most dear to the knightly heart ;

not silver or gold, not applause and popularity, but a share in all the good which those whom he has succoured shall hereafter do. *They* shall never thenceforth raise the fallen, or redeem the captive, or save the lost, but that *he* shall be accounted a fellow-worker with them, a partaker in their good deeds (ver. 8). O noble spur to a holy ambition! O large and blessed reward! Yet there is not one of us who does not enter into it so often as we " support such persons " as deny themselves to serve the truth, or help forward on his journey any brother who may be hard bested. Thenceforth we are fellow-workers with them, and through them may engage in enterprises and achieve victories beyond our strength or valour. Receive a prophet in the name of a prophet, and you shall have the prophet's reward. Receive a righteous man, because he is a righteous man, and his reward shall also be yours.

Last of all, let us mark how this Letter bears on our duties as members of the Christian fellowship. Here is a church with a vain self-confident pastor, addicted to anathemas; and a lay member who walks in the truth and is addicted to hospitality. To these there comes the good Demetrius, bearing a letter from the Apostle John (ver. 9), a letter of introduction and commendation. Demetrius, says the letter, has given himself to the service of the Gentiles, taking no wage of them lest they should suspect his motive : let all good men further him in his work. But bishop Diotrophes is not going to be dictated to by John, apostle though he be. He refuses to receive or help Demetrius ; he excommunicates any member of his church who ventures to receive this objectionable missionary. Layman Caius, on the other hand, recognizes a brother in · the stranger, loves him, and proves his love by hospitable welcome and kindly furtherance. The story is a very simple one, and has very simple lessons for us. It teaches us what are the dangers to which, as members of the Church, we are exposed. *We* may love authority, and strive for pre-eminence ; we may be jealous of brethren who interpret the Gospel on a larger method than ours, and devote themselves to duties which we have neglected : we may be impatient of guidance and control, however wise, however gentle, it may be. . And if we give place to these evil tempers, we may blacken the character of men who are better than we are, " prating malicious words " against even an apostolic spirit : we may reject those whom God has received, dishonour those whom He has honoured : we may hinder willing brethren from doing a good work to which we should incite them : and thus we may miss the large reward of being fellow-workers with all who serve the truth.

On the other hand, if we would be Christian men and gentlemen, true members of the true Church, we may, we must, make it our chief aim to serve Christ in serving our brethren, although they may hold other views than we, and adopt different modes of action, not seeking to get our own way or secure our own pre-eminence.   As we might be very well content to do, if for no better reason, yet for this : that those who seek honour selfishly hardly ever acquire it, never retain it.   I hope Diotrophes was a good man, despite his vanity, his volubility, his contempt for lawful authority.   But if he was a good

K

man, with what bitter regret must he now remember his faults, his sins against truth and love ; and if he were not, how soon his apparent victory over Demetrius was turned into lasting defeat ; how heavy his punishment in that for eighteen centuries he has been the standing illustration of what a Christian pastor should not be !

If we are the faithful servants of Christ, we shall follow Caius and Demetrius rather than Diotrophes. Because we think for ourselves, and strike out our own course, the course which God has marked out for us by the capacities He has conferred upon us, we shall love the truth, whoever may speak it ; we shall make brethren of strangers rather than strangers of brethren ; and, by virtue of a tender sympathy and ready succour, we shall seek to share in the good works of all the good. We shall use what opportunities of service are sent us, instead of sighing for other opportunities and more. We shall be considerate and helpful in our intercourse with each other, not hindering, and forbidding, and condemning : and for all honest, disinterested, misinterpreted servants of the Truth, we shall feel a very special sympathy and tenderness. Thus we shall prove that we have the spirit of Caius—nay, of Christ Himself; and associate ourselves with that noble army of every race and age, in which are ranked not only heroes and chief captains, but also a great multitude of the humble and undistinguished; and in which the Lord Christ, the Captain of our Salvation, has kept a place for every one of us, if only we care to fill it.

YATES & ALEXANDER, Printers, Church Passage, Chancery Lane.